THE BLOOD-STAINED MAN

THE BLOOD-STAINED MAN

NETHERWORLD

BOOK 2

CHRISTOPHER ROWLEY

A TOM DOHERTY ASSOCIATES BOOK

NEW YORK TOR®

 HEAVY METAL

HEAVY METAL PULP: THE BLOODSTAINED MAN: NETHERWORLD BOOK TWO

Copyright © 2010 by Heavy Metal Unloaded, LLC

A Tor Book
Published by Tom Doherty Associates, LLC
175 Fifth Avenue
New York, NY 10010

www.tor-forge.com

Design by Greg Collins

Tor® is a registered trademark of Tom Doherty Associates, LLC.

ISBN 978-0-7653-2389-7

First Edition: June 2010

THE BLOOD-STAINED MAN

#

New York City was getting hammered by the storm. Relentless rain and wind sent water firehosing along the streets.

Rook Venner, Senior Investigative Officer from the Hudson Valley Police Department, knew he was in a tough situation. All hell was going to break loose as soon as the cops found what the trio had left behind at former president Marion's penthouse.

Rook glanced down East Forty-second and saw police lights, lots of them, where the Gotham Tower loomed in the night sky. Thoughts went spinning wildly through his mind. The image of ex-president Marion's head exploding all over the luxurious penthouse apartment. The smell of fresh brains and blood. The urge to puke. Rook had ignored the man's frantic waving hands, his face turning ash-white at the words "Taste Imperative."

Not thirty-six hours ago, Rook had been a homicide detective assigned to a routine case, his biggest problem a car that wouldn't start. Now he was on the run, a rogue cop targeted by military, government black ops, and God knew what other organizations with access to big weapons, gunships, and killer robots. The key to any hope for survival were the two women who walked beside him.

He glanced at the young blonde, a gene-grown human pleasure model. Her former owner, Manuel Sangacha, was the murder victim, an ex-general with a dark past. Rook had rescued the mod on a wild hunch she was vital to the case. He was more right than he knew. He replayed in his mind the image of her spinning like a superheated top as she kicked the crap out of a full-armored tac-team. A five-foot-eight, 120-pound pleasure model shouldn't be able to do that. But Plesur had been transformed, upgraded into a fighting machine by a military earback taken from the ex-president's apartment.

"I'm soaked," the other woman complained, her ash-blond hair slicked down on either side of her face.

Rook glanced at the tall woman's leather bustier and spiked heels, not the preferred rain gear for 2068. They'd met the mysterious, leather-clad dominatrix, who went by the name Julia, at Marion's penthouse. She had paid a visit to her now ex-client looking for a different set of answers. Who had killed her fiancé twenty-five years ago, and was she still on the hit list?

Rook supposed he should be grateful. He'd thought Plesur was dead. He had left her at a clinic to get an ear-back upgrade, but the place had sold her to a local pimp. Julia had acquired Plesur for the late president.

"I thought leather was waterproof." Rook's mouth twitched in a smile.

"Not unless you're a cow!"

Three fugitives on the run, inextricably tied together by one fucked-up murder case. They had two clues: one, a set of geographical coordinates planted in Plesur's head by Sangacha. The other, a piece of a government file with the words "Taste Imperative," and four names, all of people missing or dead according to his Nokia superphone, a high-end computing device named Ingrid.

The wind gusted again, forcing them to take shelter in a doorway. A cop car went north on Third Avenue with the rack lit up.

Rook hunched deeper in the shadows. "We have to get off the street."

"Brilliant plan," Julia snapped. "Where to?"

Good question. For the first time in his life, Rook had no direction. He had been a good cop, always put the bad guys away. What was he supposed to do now? This time the bad guys were government, military—or both. It seemed someone wanted Plesur dead and someone else wanted her alive. Who was who? Freddie Beckman from Sable Ranch, the political juggernaut that had run the country for the past fifty years, had helped them, giving Rook a warning that saved his life. But whoever had tried to kill him and Plesur had used heavy military gunships. Who else but Sable Ranch had access to that kind of hardware? They were caught in the cross fire but he couldn't see who was holding the guns. How could a rogue cop, a pleasure mod, and a dominatrix crack this case? And better yet, live to write the screenplay about it.

Plesur pressed close beside him. She looked exhausted, no doubt from the adrenaline spike of her newly acquired fighting skills. Thanks to the implant gleaming behind her right ear she had taken down the tac-team sent to kill them. Rook had a handful of other implants in his pocket, taken from the ex-president's penthouse. He had no idea what they might turn Plesur into.

Rook went through the list of people who could help them. It didn't take long. The only person he trusted was his partner, Lindi MacEar, but it was too risky to contact her. Everyone thought he was dead, but by now he surely had been ID'd by the surveillance tapes in Marion's apartment. Freddie Beckman was the only other candidate, but who knew how he felt about Rook's blowing up a relative.

Suddenly the mod turned wide blue eyes to him and said, "Ronald Clampen, Lydia Trenchard."

"What?" Rook leaned forward.

"I know these names. Like the number I told you."

"Wait." Rook fished out the piece of paper he had retrieved from Sangacha's apartment. On it was the name Dr. Clampen. Seemed Sangacha had planted more than numbers in her pretty head. "We have a match."

"They can help me, us," Plesur insisted.

"That's just great, sugar." Julia shivered. "I hope they run the Four Seasons."

Rook flipped open his phone. "Say those names again," he told Plesur.

She did, and the Nokia responded instantly in its cool, female Scandinavian voice, "Two matches. Dr. Ronald Clampen, senior executive, Synodyne Genetics, California. Deceased."

"The other?"

"Lydia Trenchard, vice-presidential candidate for the Democratic Party in this year's election. Running with Paula Perez."

"What do they have to do with Sangacha?"

"Unclear. Most likely the information is triggered under crisis mode," Ingrid deduced. "Lydia Trenchard is holding a fund-raiser at the NooZoic Gallery. It's on Thirty-sixth Street, west of Fifth Avenue."

Julia glanced at the nearest street sign. They were at Park Avenue and Thirty-seventh. "That's two blocks from here."

Rook glanced at Julia. "Let's take in a little art."

Julia arched an eyebrow, glancing at the array of automatic weapons they carried. "We're a bit overdressed."

"Trash them here. Some lucky citizen can start his own revolution."

They pressed on, making their way west, the gray tower

of Grand Central Terminal looming behind them like a tomb.

Plesur gripped his arm. "Why do I know these things?"

Those incredible blue eyes were brimming over with confusion. Plesur had gone from subnormal intelligence to being like anyone else when they'd snapped that earback into the socket behind her ear. She wasn't just a pleasure model anymore. She was intelligent, trying to deal with being only three weeks old with a lifetime's worth of questions and emotions.

"Maybe Lydia Trenchard has some answers." Rook tried to sound soothing.

Another crazy gust of wind drove rain sideways across the street. The gutters were overflowing, an awning down by the corner had torn free and was flapping like the wing of some huge, captive bird.

"Come on," said Rook, pulling Plesur close to his side. "Just one more block."

They ran to the pool of light in front of the gallery. NOOZOIC read a sparkly sign across the front. The windows were pink and opaque, the people inside visible only as silhouettes. Sounds of applause and cheering drifted through the door.

"Must be the place." Rook ran a hand over his slick hair, noting he needed a trim.

A limo drew up at the curb beside them. Several people

came running out of NooZoic as the car's rear door swung open.

A massive guy in black neoprene emerged and sprouted an umbrella from one hand.

In a sudden swirl of lights, a police car shot past, heading south. The sight galvanized Rook, and he shooed Plesur into NooZoic, Julia right behind.

"God, who are these people?" Julia pushed her way through the crowd.

"Together we can take back America!"

A lady in a striped gray suit raised her arms. She stood on a podium at the rear of the gallery. She was older gen with carefully tinted auburn hair.

Applause erupted as people waved signs that read PEREZ/ TRENCHARD FOR A NEW AMERICA!

"Everyone knows what we've been through in this country. But what we want to know is, when will it be over?"

There was a good crowd, maybe 150 people. Rook noted men in high-end suits, pale gray and blue, women in ultra-fashionable tiny miniskirts and high heels. The humid air was full of expensive fragrances.

"What Paula Perez is saying," the woman continued, her voice impassioned, "and what the Democratic Party is saying, is that enough is enough. We want our country back!"

The crowd broke into prolonged applause, cheering and whistling as Lydia Trenchard stepped off the podium. She shook hands, waved to friends, accepted hugs.

Rook saw Plesur staring at the artwork exhibit. "What is it?"

"Me. . . ."

With a start Rook saw the walls were covered with large portraits of pleasure models, dozens of them. An entire row of Pammies, six foot by four, cascaded over the far wall. They seemed to move, ghost-dancing across the arid desert. On the other side of the gallery, a row of AfriQueens hypnotically swayed against the lush veld. At a distance of twenty feet each group looked identical, but as Rook drew closer, he noticed slight differences. Some were obviously older, with lines around their eyes and mouths. Some had nothing but innocence in their eyes, others had nothing but sorrow.

"So many," said Plesur, struggling with the new understanding of what she was. A genetic construct, a product, with thousands of identical models out there, all around the world, designed for one purpose.

Rook could sense her confusion and agony.

"Why so many?" she asked him.

"You're very popular."

"Life lesson number one." Julia shook rain from her hair. "Men are fucked-up."

Plesur had tears in her eyes. "I am just ... that." She pointed to the portraits.

Rook wanted to help ease the pain, he didn't really know how. "You're your own person now."

"For how long?"

"Oh my fucking Christ!"

He felt another presence at his elbow and found a gorgeous young woman wearing a way too tight sparkling silver minidress and high heels. She looked like a virt star. Her orange hair streamed down her back.

"You must be the artist," Rook surmised.

"Eve Euridiki." She circled Plesur, taking her in from top to bottom. "And you are perfection."

"Her name's Plesur."

"That's the default." Eve's eyes flicked from Julia to Plesur, then back to Rook. "You on some kind of slave fantasy trip?"

Julia laughed. "I wouldn't piss her off, if I were you."

"Plesur is smart," Rook said.

"Fan-fucking-tastic! You had an upgrade. So tell me, what do you think?" Euridiki waved a hand at the paintings of Pammies.

Plesur thought for a minute. "I am them, but then I am not."

"That is the point of my work," Eve approved. "Mods are all identical, but as they age, they change, just like we do. And yet we deny them human rights, we deny them humanity."

Suddenly Rook remembered where he'd seen the name Euridiki before.

"I've seen some of your work. A desert scene."

"My Arizona series."

"They were on the walls of Manuel Sangacha's apartment."

Euridiki's head snapped up at that name, and she focused on Rook much more intently than before.

"You know Manuel?"

"Not really." Rook bit his lip for a moment. "He's dead." He searched her eyes for a reaction. He got one.

Euridiki took a step back, shook her head. "They killed him."

"Who might 'they' be?"

"Who else, Sable Ranch."

Rook felt his eyebrows rise involuntarily. How much did this woman know? "That's the popular theory. How well did you know him?"

She gave a shrug. "Manuel was a steady client. Bought a lot of pieces. He loved art."

Rook's mouth twitched. "Who'd have guessed."

"He hid behind a lot of walls."

Yeah, Rook thought. Too bad they weren't made of lead.

The crowd parted as Lydia Trenchard strode up to Eve.

"Crowd loves you," said Eve as the two hugged. "Meet my new friends, love."

Lydia extended her hand to Rook. "Thank you for coming."

"Name's Venner, Rook. Plesur."

"The pleasure is all mine." Lydia smiled.

"My name is Plesur. I am one of those." The mod pointed to the Pammies on the wall.

Lydia's blue eyes studied Plesur. She seemed to understand everything about Plesur in an instant. "But you're a little different, aren't you?"

"I am smart now."

"That's wonderful, dear."

"This is Julia," Rook said.

"Hello." Lydia Trenchard stared at her for a moment. "I meet the most interesting people at these events."

A young lady appeared with a tray of champagne flutes brimming with bubbles. Lydia downed one and took a second.

Eve tugged on Lydia's jacket and bent her head down.

". . . belonged to the general," was all that Rook heard.

"My God." Lydia Trenchard stared at Plesur.

"Sangacha planted your name in her head," Rook told the politician.

Lydia stepped close to the mod. "Do you have a message for me?"

"Just this, 74 17 06 97."

"Location coordinates, interesting." Lydia's steel blue eyes focused on Rook. "Who the hell are you?"

"The information she carries is vital to my case."

"Perhaps the entire country." Lydia paused. "You sound like a cop."

Rook flushed. "I am, was, a cop. Homicide detective."

"But not anymore."

"Recently dead. I was assigned the Sangacha murder."

Lydia looked behind her, then leaned close to him. "So you know he was Louisa Marion's hatchet man."

"You mean the ISS."

Lydia's eyes went wide. "You've been busy, Detective."

Just then, one of her handlers interrupted, handing her a phone.

"What?" Lydia said. "Arkansas?"

Rook felt pressure on his left thigh. Plesur was standing close to him. She took his hand, anxiety clear in her eyes.

"What is happening?"

"Not sure."

Plesur tugged on Rook's sleeve. "Lights outside."

Rook looked down the gallery to the pink, opaque window. Police lights were flashing. Men in tac suits were piling out of squad cars. Rook's heart sank. He turned back to Eve Euridiki. "We have to get out of here."

Her eyes flicked to the front doors. "Why?"

Rook shook his head grimly. "Somebody's trying to kill us."

"Get the fuck out!" Euridiki was immediately excited.

"The mod must be saved at all costs," Lydia said. Noting the apprehension in Rook's eyes, she glanced at Eve. "I have a feeling this party is about to get a lot more interesting."

Wheels spun in the artist's head for a moment and she made a quick decision. "Game on."

A sudden disturbance at the front door caused heads to turn.

Julia eyed the commotion. "We must have been picked by CCTV on the street."

"Come with me." Lydia spun on an immaculate heel and shouted orders to her staff. "Rosie, call Hugo. Set up a switch. Let's go, now!"

Her handlers were moving toward the back of the gallery. Eve Euridiki was shoving people out of the way. "Hurry!"

Bright lights blazed at the door, and suddenly armored tac suits were pushing inside. People ran screaming into the back of the gallery.

Rook met Julia's raised eyebrow. What choice did they have? With Plesur following, they were back on the run.

CHAPTER 2

They hurried through the back office of the gallery away from the sounds of screams and things being smashed.

"You break it, you bought it!" Eve shouted, flinging open the doors to the rain-soaked alley. A green sedan was waiting in a narrow, brick-lined space.

"Get in!" Lydia slid into the passenger seat as Eve jumped behind the wheel. The other three piled in the back.

The doors closed, the car started. "Plan B," Lydia said in a firm voice, and the car, a Mercedes M-type Kombidrive, leaped forward like a sprinter out of the blocks.

Rook saw the brick wall fly by, inches from his face, and

flinched. Plesur seemed nonplussed as Eve sprang open the glove compartment and tossed her a sleek handgun.

"Here ya go, Killa."

Plesur cocked the chamber as the car hurtled into the street and hung a sharp right, going over on two wheels. With a shriek of rubber, the Mercedes gunned itself to the end of the block. "Great car, huh?" Eve said.

"Programmed to override the rails, nice." Rook was jammed back into the plush seats like a baseball into a catcher's glove.

"Listen closely," said Lydia. "We're going to switch cars in a few seconds. Only way to beat the surveillance." She saw Rook's look in the driver's mirror and went on, "We do it all the time."

The car screamed off the avenue and dove into a parking garage, plunged down two levels, and slammed to a halt with barely a foot to spare in front of a white-painted brick wall.

"Later, babe." Eve leaned over and kissed Lydia, then scrambled out, heading for a white van.

Plesur and Julia climbed out of the back just as someone else dove into the driver's seat, backed the car up, spun it around, and rocketed up a ramp.

Meanwhile a black Gaoshu had appeared from around another corner. The doors popped open.

"Let's go," said Lydia.

They piled in and were off.

Exiting the parking garage on the other side of the block, they moved sedately down to the light, then turned and rolled north. The Gaoshu was a luxury model out of Shanghai, popular with politicians everywhere because it was routinely bulletproofed.

"Your constituents know you drive like this?" asked Rook after a block or two.

Lydia arched an eyebrow. "I'm not the vice president yet."

"Rough competition." Rook craned his neck to check for pursuers.

"Exactly," Lydia agreed.

They continued across town on Thirty-sixth Street. Behind them, police lights streaked across the slick avenues.

"You know the senior senator from Texas?" Rook asked.

"We've met. Louisa Marion is a very dangerous person, thinks what she does is all for the good of the nation."

Rook snorted. "Doesn't every politician?"

"You mean like me?" Lydia asked wryly. "People have stopped paying attention to politics. But Paula is getting noticed. She's tough, fearless, and believe me, Sable Ranch is running scared."

"I can see why," Rook quipped.

Julia spoke up from the backseat. "Musical cars part of the campaign strategy?"

"Sable Ranch has been killing people for forty years; they're good at it."

Lydia punched coordinates into the computer and the car careened from West Thirty-sixth Street onto the West Side Highway. They barreled north, Manhattan towers looming on their right.

"Paula won't let Marion continue to operate as she does now," Lydia said.

Rook felt deeply uneasy. He had never heard anyone talk about Sable Ranch like this. You could get in serious trouble that way.

The car swooped along the on-ramp to the George Washington Bridge. The lights along the mighty spans of steel crossing the Hudson River gleamed in the rain. Clouds obscured the New Jersey side, where the uninsured regions lay hidden like lost worlds.

"Who do *you* think killed the general?" Rook asked Trenchard.

"Nobody could get to him while he was protected by Sable Ranch."

The Gaoshu accelerated sharply, pressing them back into the seats as it hit two hundred miles an hour for the straight run across the bridge.

Rook glimpsed something from the corner of his eye and grabbed the wheel, pulling it hard. The dash lit up with a warning light, a robot voice blared, "Improper procedure, desist!" The car jumped the rails to the inside lane, horns blaring behind them.

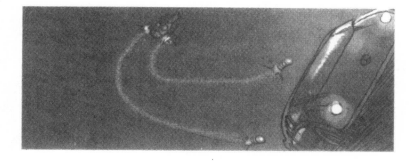

Something bright, white, and loud exploded exactly where they would've been.

"Fuck!" Julia screamed as the entire bridge shook from the impact.

A shadow zoomed overhead—Rook caught the flash of a flying silver rocket—skimming around in an arc.

"Keep weaving, get into the tunnel for Route 4," Rook instructed.

"What the fuck was that?" Lydia hit the control panel. The Gaoshu whipped to the outside lane, rocketing past surrounding traffic.

"Military drone," Rook snarled. "Fired a missile at us."

"A military drone?" Lydia glanced back at Plesur, astonished. "Those coordinates must be pretty important."

"They've been trying to kill her for days," Rook confirmed.

"Jesus, how do they know?"

Plesur was looking out the back window. "They're smart too."

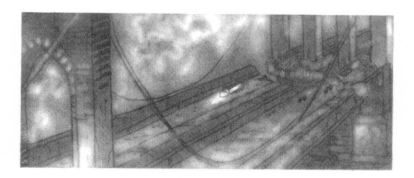

Dark dots were rapidly growing larger in the side-view mirror.

"Motorcycles," Rook shouted.

But the dots had overtaken them, slotting in from their right. Sleek, black predatory vehicles moving with all the fury of a jet engine. The guy on the second bike was leveling a tube at them.

"Look out!" Rook pulled Lydia down by the shoulders.

The Gaoshu rocked from the blast, slamming against the guardrail, almost flipping over and into roiling waters thirty stories below. The big car came back down on all four wheels with a violent hammering. The guy on the second bike was hosing the car with a submachine gun.

It sounded like demons battering the Gaoshu with

hammers, but the armor was good enough. Frustrated, the biker fired another grenade shell. The side windows exploded like powder.

Automatic gunfire exploded in the car. Plesur hung out the window unloading a full clip. They hurtled off the bridge and down into the tunnel leading to Route 4.

The first motorcycle accelerated, leaping up to the outer rail and coming up fast beside them. The shooter changed clips. Now he would simply execute them while they cowered inside the car.

Rook leaned out to nail the shooter. But before he could pull the trigger, the guy swerved his bike sharply, crushing the back of Rook's wrist. To Rook's horror, he lost the gun. For a split second he saw it, tumbling, about to fall, until a delicate hand snatched it out of the air with a speed beyond human and fired. The guy flew backward, firing as he went, stitching a line of bullets into the ceiling tiles on the tunnel.

Plesur flipped the gun and shot the second assassin. He fell, dragging the machine off the rail. It exploded against the tunnel wall, and the Gaoshu, battered, but still rolling, broke out of the fireball and into the rain-lashed night air.

Lydia pulled the wheel hard, the car rocked as it shifted left into another lane. Up ahead an exit promised access to Route 17 and Paramus. Apartment towers were all around, lights blurry through the rain.

With the windshield gone they were all soaked in seconds, and the wind was ramming them back into the upholstery.

Plesur leaned forward with an effort and handed Rook the gun, her eyes unreadable in the dark.

"Thanks," Lydia said. "Saved all our lives."

Plesur smiled. "Killa earback."

With a bump and a rattle the Gaoshu left the rail. The hybrid engine purred to life, automatically taking over.

Then Rook noticed the wing lights of something flying low, just beyond the nearest apartment towers.

"Drone is still on us. We have to get under some kind of cover."

The drone swung around a gleaming office tower, dropped down to about a hundred feet off the ground, and shot straight at them.

"Look out!" Lydia spun the wheel. The Gaoshu jumped the curb, landing in the tower's driveway and smashed through a barrier to the underground parking.

Behind them everything went white. The ground shook and the car was thrown forward, caroming off the side wall of the down ramp. Glass was smashed and stripped off the building above, hitting the street with a long roar.

Julia screamed as a piece of glass the size of a door slammed into the back of the car.

Superb Chinese engineering, plus a little luck, saved them. The car didn't flip over as it boomed out onto the lower floor.

Lydia braked, popped the doors. They got out, shaking.

"We don't have much time," said Rook.

They left the Gaoshu where it was. Lydia went for the elevator, but Rook pulled her away.

"They can track that. We have to get into the walls."

"What?" said Lydia.

Rook was looking back at the dark well of the ramp. A red laser beam flicked on the wall. He pulled open the door to the fire stairs and pushed Plesur inside.

"Up?" Plesur asked.

"No. Down."

Lydia seemed unconvinced.

"They're already upstairs," said Rook. "Believe me, I know what they're doing. There's a tac-squad here, must have been right behind us on the bridge."

Lydia whipped out her phone. "This has gone too far. When Paula hears of this—"

"Tell her later." Rook was concentrating on more immediate matters. Like staying alive.

"Cell phones suck!" Lydia's voice rang in the stairwell.

Rook handed Lydia his Nokia. "Meet Ingrid."

They went down a level.

Lydia punched a few buttons on Ingrid's screen. "It's telling me to hold it against the pipes."

"Do it." Rook stayed at the foot of the stairs, sidearm ready. "And it's a she." The Nokia knew what was required to make phone calls from any place on earth, even the moon, probably.

Placing one end of the phone against the pipes, Lydia dialed. "Patsy? We've got trouble. I'm in Fort Lee somewhere. Get me a ride. You got the position? Hurry, this is not a drill."

Lydia hung up and handed Ingrid back to Rook. "Gotta get me one of these."

"Worth the money." Rook heard boots rasping on concrete above them. "Let's go."

This was a modern building; there would be engineering adits and shafts in two corners of the lot. Rook had been on at least seven homicide cases where bodies had been hidden in such shafts and deep passages. In one famous case, in Kingston Waterside, a man had killed his wife and built a false wall at the bottom of a shaft and concreted it to look like the rest. Solving that one had built Rook's early reputation.

He led the others along the wall. "Keep your heads down," he whispered.

In the corner, as expected, was a blue door. Locked, of course, but with a numeric pad.

"Do your thing, baby." Rook connected the Nokia to the little port at the base of the lock.

They stood there anxiously until the lock emitted a soft clunk. Rook pulled the door open.

"After you."

As he closed it behind himself, he saw the first red laser beams of the tac-squad appear from the doorway to the fire stairs.

Their presence had activated dim ceiling lightstrips, enough to show a narrow passage.

"Where are we?" asked Lydia.

"Seismic study shaft," Rook said. "All new buildings above a certain size have them. Lets them see if anything's changing."

As expected, halfway along Rook found a vertical shaft with steel rungs set into the concrete.

"Goes all the way to the roof," said Rook. "Climb, and make it quick. They won't take long to figure out where we've gone."

"Jesus, what a day," said Lydia.

"Beats fund-raising, I'm sure." Julia managed a quick grin.

They climbed, with Plesur leading and Rook bringing up the rear. When they reached the upper parking area, they found another narrow passageway. They entered just as they heard the door down below blow open and a voice shout, "Move it!"

"Run!" said Rook in a harsh whisper.

They scrambled down the narrow passage to its end.

It seemed like just a blind alley. Lights were shining up from the shaft and they could hear boots on the metal rungs. Rook knew that if he was wrong about this, they were going to die.

"Shit," he muttered.

"There's nowhere to go," said Julia. "We're trapped."

Rook used the Nokia's flashlight, saw the bolts set into the seven-foot-high ceiling.

"Hold the light." He gave it to Julia and climbed.

"What are you doing?" said Lydia.

"This is an inspection trap. Exits behind the building."

"Man, you got mad skills for a cop," said Julia as Rook pulled the bolts.

The bolts came out, Rook pressed his shoulder to the trap. The damned thing was stuck, had probably never been opened before.

"I think you should hurry," said Lydia. "They're—"

Her words were cut short by a shriek of steel as the trapdoor finally gave it up and popped open. Rook scrambled onto the street. They were at the rear of the building, on the edge of a concrete pan where runoff water rushed down to a massive drain. He reached back and pulled Julia out.

"Jesus," said Julia, climbing the narrow rungs. "What are these designed for, chipmunks?"

Gunfire broke out below them.

"Fuck!" Rook grabbed Lydia's arms and tossed her onto the concrete. Bullets were ricocheting around Plesur as she sprang to the surface, ready for action. She kicked the trapdoor shut as bullets punched through it.

"Are you okay?" Rook gave her a once-over.

Plesur dusted herself off. "Fine, you?"

"Come on," he said, pushing Lydia ahead of him. They peered around the corner to the main street.

They found a scene of devastation. The missile strike

had stripped half the glass off the front of the building. A hose company battled a first-floor blaze and paramedics were loading gurneys into waiting ambulances.

A big white Mercedes limo burst through the smoke. "That's us. Let's go," said Lydia.

Behind them they heard shouts, the tac-team was coming.

The limo's doors popped open.

"Upgrade," said Rook, pushing Plesur inside.

"You bet," said Lydia.

In the driver's seat was a mean-looking teenager.

"Ready?" The kid revved the massive engine.

"Paco, get us the fuck out of here," Lydia ordered.

"Yes, ma'am."

Paco gunned the motor and sent the big car flying onto the side street, dodging a pile of smashed black glass, then hurtled onto the main road.

"Sable Ranch isn't exactly keeping a low profile," Julia observed.

"Never seen them this desperate before," said Lydia. "It's refreshing."

"So is staying alive," Rook snorted.

The big limo bounced across a four-lane highway, straight into a gas station that looked as if it had been out of business for twenty years. Paco spun the wheel and they swung around to the back and ground to a halt.

Eve Euridiki was there, back doors of a van wide-open.

"You're late!" she shouted at them from the driver's seat. "Move!"

Ten seconds later, the van bumped through a chain-link fence at the back of the gas station, swerved through an empty lot strewn with tires, then took off down a suburban street with a screech of rubber.

"Did we lose them?" Julia wondered, peering back through the glass in the van doors.

"Are you dead?" Eve asked.

"No."

"Okay, then, nice job." Eve smiled.

Eve brought the van out on a commercial strip and they slid into railed traffic riding the midspeed.

Seconds slid by, Rook kept watching the dark sky, looking for red wing lights, but they didn't show, and slowly, very slowly, his pulse came down from panic attack to something closer to normal.

"We escaped." Plesur grinned.

"That's one way of describing it," said Lydia.

"At least we know something now," said Rook.

"Life is one fucked-up shithole?" asked Julia.

"Whatever it is Plesur knows, they're ready to kill a lot of people to keep it a secret."

CHAPTER 3

The ride through the New Jersey night was tense, with Rook expecting more attacks at any moment. The rain continued to pound down on the land, but they had slipped off the assassins' radar screen. Eve kept them on a midspeed rail as they passed under highway 287 amid lots of other traffic.

Maybe it was the lack of sleep, just a few hours out of the past forty-eight, or maybe it was all the adrenaline, the tension, the fear, but Rook felt drained, shaky, barely able to think straight.

Plesur had sunk into obvious exhaustion. She rested her head on Rook's chest, and in about five minutes she was

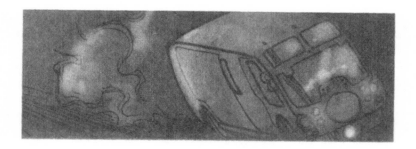

fast asleep. Rook studied her perfect face, the silver ear-back flashing through her golden hair. What would it feel like to have your IQ suddenly jump fifty points? Through everything, Plesur had remained calm and composed. Was it just the upgrade, or was that poise unique to her?

Julia was brooding, staring out the rear window of the van as the suburban landscape slid past, veiled by rain. Huge pools flooded the road, slowing traffic to a crawl.

After a while, it became clear that they had given their attackers the slip. The tension began to subside. Rook finally took his right hand off the sidearm.

Lydia turned to check on her passengers. She smiled at the sleeping mod. "Secret's safe for now."

"How did you know Sangacha?" Rook asked.

"I knew him indirectly, you could say."

"Oh?"

Euridiki intervened. "Lydia was in the camps."

Rook turned back to Lydia. "I'm sorry."

"That was a long time ago. I've done all right. Senator from New Jersey for two terms, don't suppose you remember that."

"I'm not political."

"That's one of the problems in our country."

"Does the Ranch know?" said Rook.

"I went in as one person and came out as another, married to someone else. I've covered my tracks since then but you can never be sure."

Julia turned away from the rear window and spoke in a voice tinged with urgency and something else, possibly regret. "Why did they put you in the camps?"

Lydia sighed. "My husband Jack and me, we were active against the war. At that point it had been going on for nearly twenty-five years. We thought the U.S. should try something else."

She paused, then gestured in the air with one hand. "We've been fighting in the Middle East for more than sixty years. Did it ever occur to anyone that maybe we're doing something wrong?"

"My fiancé was a soldier," Julia said. "Said we had to fight to keep our freedom."

"That's the official excuse. Didn't work. Our government took away our freedom, not the terrorists'."

They digested that thought in silence for a while.

Then Lydia said, "We were liberals, so they arrested us. That was Minnesota during the winter of 2031. I never saw my husband again."

"Where did they send you?" said Rook.

"Women's Camp D, Montana. I was twenty-four years old, and I was pretty. So I got lucky. I wound up in a brothel for higher-ranking officers with a few hundred others."

Rook had heard about the camps, but they always seemed like myths. Secret prisons during the Emergency where anyone who spoke out against Sable Ranch was taken and never heard from again.

"That's where I met General Sangacha."

Plesur shifted back to awareness, eyes glinting at the mention of her former owner's name.

"He introduced me to General Steve Lawrence," Lydia continued. "I wound up marrying him."

Rook shook his head. This lady had one hell of a story.

"A week later they took the girls away, all of them."

"Where?" Julia asked.

"I don't know." Lydia sighed. "Steve got drunk one night and told me they were killed, every single one of them. Next morning, he woke up and put a bullet into his brain."

"Sorry," Julia murmured.

"He was an arrogant bastard. Hated the sight of him."

"They killed Mark in '44," Julia said. "I've been running ever since."

"What's your connection to Sangacha?"

"He hired me to whip him."

"Ha!" Eve snorted. "So the old fuck had some kind of conscience."

They fell silent again, aware of the huge forces that were arrayed against them. Staying alive seemed less and less likely every time Rook thought about it.

Plesur was trying to focus. "I wish I knew more."

"There are ways to change that," Eve said.

The van shifted across the rails to an exit. Weeds and dense clumps of bamboo lined the ramp. At the bottom a traffic light swung uselessly over a T-junction.

The left turn ended in a wall of concrete blocks and chain-link fence standing in pools of dirty brown water. On the other side of the fence was uninsured territory. A dilapidated panorama of ruined apartment blocks, crumbling walls, rooms open to the sky. Weed trees grew thickly over abandoned forecourts. Rook noticed a hole ripped in the chain links and deep ruts in the dirt. The uninsured could never completely be walled out.

The right turn took them past a ruined strip mall, then to a zone of commercial buildings, standing in a row beside a four-lane highway. A pair of huge, twenty-six-wheel automatic tractor-trailers were just pulling out through a gate in front of a warehouse. Beside the gate, armed guards were visible in the rain.

"Where are we?" asked Julia.

"This is Spillside, wrong side of the highway from Lincoln Park," said Eve.

"Looks like a war zone," said Julia.

"Uninsured space over there." Rook indicated the west and south with a sweep of his hand. "Unless you've got good policing here, it's gonna be dangerous."

"I pay the local Latins for protection," said Euridiki. "That's worked so far."

The van swept past a couple more large buildings, all fronted by chain-link fencing with razor wire on top, and pulled up at another gate at the end of the line. A moment later the gate slid open and the van rolled inside and stopped beside the covered loading dock of a small warehouse.

"Okay, we're here," said Lydia, opening her door.

The rain was still hammering down. Sheets of water were gushing off the roof of the building and flowing away into the dark.

Rook climbed down, gave a hand to Plesur, and she joined him under the metal portico.

"Welcome to my hovel," said Eve, waving a remote key at the front doors.

Inside, the spacious warehouse was stuffed with Euridiki's art. Paintings lined the walls. Sculptures made from a variety of "found" materials were stashed toward the back.

"Got a lot of stuff in here," Rook observed.

"Ten years' worth of art productions."

"Must be worth a lot of money."

"Don't touch anything."

Rook found Plesur staring at paintings of pleasure models. About half of them were Pammies, just like her.

"Where do we come from?" Her blue eyes filled with concern.

Rook shrugged. "I don't know."

"You came from Santz Laboratories in Manila." Eve Euridiki sauntered over, handing Rook a turkey micro dinner. "Huge operation now, finance is fifty percent American. They have complete political cover from the Philippine government. I mean, they own the government."

"I don't have a mother," said Plesur in a sad voice.

"In a way," Eve told her. "She died a long time ago."

"Who was she?"

"Her name was Pamela, and she was very famous."

"Why?"

Eve stuck a micro dinner in the mod's hands. "Because she was beautiful, like you."

Plesur's eyes sparkled again. "Like me."

Rook blinked. Plesur had a lot of difficult discoveries ahead of her, but he knew he could do nothing to keep her from those particular truths.

With a soft chime to warn him, the Nokia spoke up.

"There is a call from Lindi MacEar."

"Secure line?"

"Uncertain."

Rook agonized for a second or two. Then he picked up the call.

"MacEar, is this secured?"

"Think so, boss. I'm using my boyfriend's old cell. I've got a few minutes before they come looking for me."

"They?"

"Christ, boss, things were really great when you were dead. Your buddy Agent Skelsa came back today. They took over the station."

"Watching your every move?"

"They got that robot right in the lobby."

Rook resisted the urge to chuckle.

"Artoli must be enjoying that."

"Get this. There's a military rebellion going on in Georgia and Arkansas. Something called the Freedom League."

"Just another fringe group."

"They put up a list of what they call 'traitors to America.' Mostly politicians and military guys, including our vic."

"What are you saying, they killed him?"

"Who knows."

"Gimme a call if you hear anything more."

"Where are you?"

"Somewhere in New Jersey. It's been a very crazy night so far."

"Be careful, boss."

The others were sitting around the table at the back of the space eating their meals. Eve and Plesur were talking, Lydia was making phone calls, and Julia sat quietly, lost in introspection.

Rook approached Lydia and sat down.

"Just talked to my partner. Looks like someone's making quite an effort to find me and Plesur."

"I'm not surprised," said Lydia. "Louisa Marion kills anyone who gets in her way. She's already feeling pressure from extremists in the south. That'll be crushed. Like the others before it. She still controls the army. But, the west is going to vote for Paula and me. So . . ." Lydia paused and glanced down the table at Plesur.

"Whatever's in Plesur's head must be pretty damned important," Rook finished the thought.

"Okay, let's see what we got." Lydia took out her phone

and projected a holo map. "These coordinates Sangacha gave you, Plesur, did he tell you what was there?"

"No. He kept me in a cage." Her eyes flashed fire for a moment, then cooled.

Sangacha had had plenty of blood on his hands, but he'd been decent enough when it came to Plesur. Sangacha had never touched the mod. She was still a virgin. For some reason that was important to Rook Venner.

"Upstate New York," Lydia mused, zooming in on the holo map. The coordinates showed thick forest bordering a mountain range with several finger lakes breaking up the mass of trees. A concrete building was barely visible through the branches. "I have no idea why Manuel thought this location was so important."

The domme looked over at the map, surprise flashing across her dark blue eyes.

"You recognize this place?" asked Rook.

Julia shrugged, her expression suddenly closed. "What's the big secret, it's just the old aqueduct."

"That's exactly what those fuckers want you to think," Eve said, spearing the last bite of her turkey dinner and waving her fork in the air. "The last place you'd look, that's the first place they'll go."

"And we have to figure out how to get there." Rook tried to calculate the distance. Not far, but it might as well be across the freakin' world when every military and law enforcement agent in the country would be looking for them.

"Whatever Louisa Marion is up to, it was enough to push Manuel over the edge," Lydia said grimly. "It can't be good."

"We have to stop it," Plesur said, beginning to understand her true importance for the first time.

Lydia smiled at the mod with admiration. "Manuel was wise to choose you."

"Smart guy," Rook agreed.

Lydia's phone beeped and she shut off the holo map. "My ride is here. I have to get back to work. Fund-raising breakfast and I can't show up in last night's suit."

"Careful out there, baby." Eve kissed her soundly.

"I'll see what I can find on this location." Lydia caressed a lock of her lover's fiery hair as she got up.

A pair of bodyguards came into the warehouse, ready to escort the politician.

"It won't be easy," Lydia said, looking from Rook to Plesur to Julia. "But we are going to save this country."

"Never thought I'd be Paul fucking Revere," said Julia.

"A new look might suit you." Lydia smiled as she walked out with the bodyguards, leaving Rook, Julia, and Plesur alone with the artist.

"You can bunk here," said Eve. She dug out blankets and even found some cushions to use as pillows. "I have some blankets and stuff." She waved to a raised platform on one side of the warehouse.

Rook made himself comfortable, then found Plesur sitting beside him.

He propped himself up on the pillows. "How're you doing?"

"I understand many things now."

He saw tears in her eyes.

"You were good to me, Rook. Thank you."

"Yeah, well, life's not fair, but in your case it seemed worse than usual."

To his relief, she understood what he was trying to say, and her smile carried sadness and forgiveness in equal measure. "I wish I could remember more."

"You're luckier than most."

"Lucky I know how to kill a man with one kick."

"That did come in handy." Rook grinned.

"You funny man," she whispered. Then her frown returned. "I thought smart would be good."

"It is. It's just that earback we picked up back there. It's not like the usual kind. Wasn't the plan."

"The 0428 D series—Bakbraka. Killa." She lay down and put her head on his chest.

Rook was too tired to protest. Plesur deserved whatever comfort she could find. Euridiki killed the lights and he was asleep in seconds.

CHAPTER 4

A volley of thunder dragged Rook into consciousness. He rolled over on the hard floor, sending a riot of aches through his tired body, and tried to ignore the storm.

"Open up, *chica!*"

Rook sprang to his feet, sidearm in hand. That wasn't thunder. Someone was banging on the metal door of Eve's warehouse. Someone who was very pissed off.

"Shit." Eve stood up from her bedroll, wild orange hair fanning around her head like a wounded phoenix.

"Friends of yours?" Rook asked.

"Sounds like the Latins."

"Didn't know they made wake-up calls." Julia looked cool and composed, unruffled by the night.

Rook moved Plesur and Julia back into the shadows, then nodded to Eve. "Get rid of them."

Eve went over to the door. "What the fuck do you want?"

"Open the fucking door."

"What if I don't?"

"How about we burn the fuckin' place down?"

"Welcome." Eve unbolted the latch and five men pushed inside, sawed-off shotguns cocked and ready. "Listen, fucktard, this is protected space, I pay Zato himself."

"Who do you think we work for?" the leader sneered.

Rook had seen guys like this before. Mirrors, polished steel, and God knows what else surgically implanted into their faces. An unsettling mosaic of scars and light, they resembled surrealistic machinery as much as men.

"You! Step out where we can see you!" the leader shouted, pointing a shotgun at Rook.

Rook held his arm out to keep Plesur behind him, but she wasn't there. Shit. The Latins were all armed to the teeth.

A figure moved like a shadow behind the five men.

Rook held his breath. Fast as lightning, Plesur kicked the largest guy behind the knees, felling him like a redwood. Completing her spin, she threw a punch to another's throat.

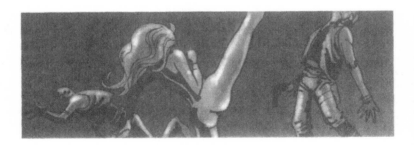

The first guy swung around, gun trained on Plesur. She kicked it aside, but before she could make another move, a sixth guy stepped from the shadows and grabbed Plesur's arm.

She cried out, her pain echoing sharply off the high metal ceiling.

"Leave her alone!" Rook lunged forward, but a wall of muscles and tattoos held him back.

The gangster grinned. "I got an upgrade, too."

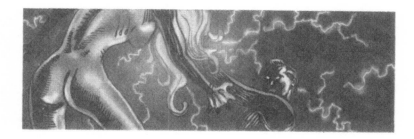

The power glove on his right hand dug into Plesur's flesh with metal fingers that increased his strength tenfold.

Electrical sparks sizzled over her body as she went down in a heap. His left hand shot out and plucked the earback from the socket behind her right ear.

Without the earback, Plesur was just a pleasure model, submissive, substandard intelligence. She struggled in the grip of her captor, screaming as he slapped her across the face, hard.

He held the earback up like a prize. "Fuckin' ay! I think we found the mod."

"Good work, Rico," the leader said, pushing Rook and Julia beside Plesur.

The one called Rico was the youngest of the group, with only a small collection of mirrors and metal decorating his sullen face.

"You must be Mr. Policeman," he sneered, flexing the power glove. One good punch from that and Rook's head would be taking a vacation from his body.

Rook didn't say anything.

"Rook?" Plesur's bright blue eyes were glazed with fear and confusion.

"It's okay, Plesur," Rook soothed. "You'll be okay."

"The gun, *ése*," said the leader, keeping his sawed-off trained on Rook's chest. Rook hesitated, but they would all die here if he opened fire. There were just too many of them.

"You want me, fine." Rook handed over his sidearm. "Leave the others alone."

"You don't give the orders no more, dickhead." The leader pocketed Rook's gun and frisked him for anything else. "Earbacks and a phone. And this."

He crumpled a piece of paper and threw it to the floor. "More garbage." He grinned at his men. *"Vámanos."*

The Latins shoved Rook, Julia, and Plesur to the door.

"Wait, you can't just take them." Eve grabbed Rico's arm.

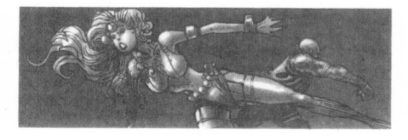

Rico slapped Eve aside. "You want this place torched?"

"No."

"Then shut the fuck up."

Rook caught Eve's gaze and nodded to the paper. He smiled gratefully. "Don't get involved. This isn't your fight."

She blinked in response.

A camouflage van pulled up to the front door. Rook counted at least three other sets of headlights outside the warehouse.

Rook guided Plesur into the back of the van, trying to keep the Latins away from her. His shins bashed the bumper as Rico shoved him harshly from behind.

"Get in, policeman." Rico's eyes flashed, taking in Julia for the first time. The domme ignored him and climbed into the van.

"Epa! Qué 'sada?" Rico slapped Julia on the ass.

Julia looked as if she wanted to kick her bootheel into his brain, but the domme moved woodenly inside the van.

The van was an antique, now supercharged with a huge engine and balloon tires. The back was stripped down to the well-worn floor, a crude metal partition separating them from the driver. The door slammed and a few seconds later the van rumbled to life and rolled out, back into the rain and down a muddy track into the uninsured side of New Jersey.

Stripped of her earback, Plesur had been reduced to a terrified silence. She sat beside Rook, staring out the side window at the rain lashing the jungle of bamboo and neotropical weed trees.

"Who are these new bunch of assholes?" asked Julia in a tense voice as they bounced through vegetation that scraped the sides of the truck and blocked the view.

"Local chapter of the Frente Nacional Latino," Rook said. "The Latins. Control these parts of the uninsured world."

"What are they going to do with us?"

That was the question that really worried Rook. "Somebody put a call out for us. Pretty sure it isn't the same people who attacked us before."

"Why do you say that?"

"Why send metalheads if you've got high-tech military tracking drones?"

The van lurched onto an old concrete roadbed, smoothing out the ride to a random jostling.

Dawn illuminated an apocalyptic panorama better left in the dark. The bones of a forgotten city jutted from the swamps, rotting roofs of tract homes squashed beside a filthy McDonald's sign. The entire landscape here was dark, without electricity.

"I didn't think it was really like this," Julia murmured.

The truck was on an elevated section of highway, below them was a lake.

"First trip on the wrong side of the tracks?" Rook asked.

Julia nodded. "Jesus, what happened here?"

"This whole area lost insurance when the water rose. The government walled it off and tried to ignore it." Rook peered through the rain. "Doing a fine job."

The van rocked as it hit a pothole, slamming Plesur's head against the wall.

"You okay?" Rook cradled the frightened mod in his arms.

"Where go?" she asked.

He saw her struggle with the question, unable to comprehend what was happening. The earback had made the simple mod he met three days ago seem like a distant memory, but her intelligence had only been temporary.

"Everything's going to be okay," he reassured her.

The van rolled slowly past the remains of box stores and chain restaurants that had been built on the river's floodplain. The shining body of a python coiled around a Starbucks sign.

"There's something up ahead." Julia pointed out the small side window to a pair of boxy towers.

This appeared to be their destination.

Rook shifted, trying to get a better view out the dirty window. "Looks like a housing project."

The van rattled over a rickety wooden bridge with

rushing brown water just a few feet below and pulled through a crowd of people in party mode despite the early hour. The smell of cooking meat wafted from large sheds that protected bright cooking fires from the rain.

The engine cut off and Rico pulled the doors open. He leered at Julia. "Time to meet the wizard."

Gun-toting thugs, faces glittering with implants and mirrors, hustled them out through the doors.

Rook walked as close as he could to Plesur as the gang took them into what had once been the lobby of the building. A row of men, chained together at the neck, were lined up along a much heavier chain.

"What on earth?" muttered Julia as they were pushed past the chain gang and forced into a battered elevator car without doors.

There was a whistle, accompanied by the crack of a whip, and the prisoners moved, hauling the chain forward and raising the elevator.

"Look at these poor bastards," Julia breathed.

Rook had to agree, but then the slaves disappeared from view as their elevator car inched slowly up the tower.

The floors along the way slowly changed. The lower levels were full of teenagers in fading clothes and crude alligator-skin jackets. Flickering candles illuminated the long, crowded hallways, some people sleeping, some passed out, some dead for all Rook cared.

"*Qué pasada!*" the kids shouted, whistling and hooting at Plesur and Julia.

These visions of hell faded as they rose up the tower and were replaced with electric lights, carpeted hallways, and freshly painted walls.

The elevator lurched to a stop as they reached their destination. A floor with deep-pile rugs and bright murals of a vaguely Mexican style on the walls, done in a skilled hand, lay before them.

"Christ, what is this?" Julia murmured.

"This is where I live." Rico leaned in close to the domme, grinning with a ripple of glinting steel.

He led them down the hall, through double doors of white wood, and into a large space, where walls had been removed. There were lights here, and every kind of electronic device, all running on micro fuel cells.

A man was waiting, surrounded by a group of his henchmen. He was clad in finely tailored alligator-skin pants, covered in tattoos and a galaxy of face implants, including a stainless-steel spike through his nose. When he smiled, silver canines gleamed in his upper jaw.

"Found them at the artist's warehouse, just like you said, *jefe*," Rico bragged.

"*Sí.*" The leader flipped a hand covered in rings, then sized up Rook. "Welcome to my *casa, amigo.* I am Zato."

Zato meant to terrify, and, Rook thought to himself, he probably did. Vermin like Zato were exactly what kept people from the insured world on their side of the fences.

Rook kept his face immobile and matched the gang leader's stare with his own.

Zato's gaze returned to Rico, then settled salaciously on Julia.

"This one. Rico, she's yours."

Julia snarled. "I don't belong to anyone."

Rico grabbed her by the hair. "Now you do."

Zato stood, casually pulled a gun from his jacket and leveled it at Rook's head. "Lotta people want you dead, policeman." He flipped the safety off.

Rook clenched his jaw.

"But I think you deserve an interesting death." Zato lowered the gun. "You put on a good fight, everyone gets to enjoy your visit, eh?"

Rico laughed. "You go to *la jaula,* the cage."

Rook understood now what all the lights on the roof were about.

Zato beckoned to Plesur. "Put her in lockdown." She shrank against Rook's side until she was torn away by the guard and shoved over to Zato.

"Don't touch her," Rook growled, struggling in the grip of two thugs.

"*Cállate.*" Zato waved his hand.

A collar was put on Julia's neck, a leash was attached, and Rico dragged her out of the room. A general murmur of grim amusement arose from the Latins.

Rook was pulled up a flight of whitewashed concrete steps and out onto the roof.

The rain was fizzling out, skies were gray, and the scene was dismal. Rows of benches surrounded a fighting ring about thirty feet across. Four giant screens were hung from scaffolding around the arena.

Debris from the night before lay everywhere. Empty bottles of beer and tequila, cigarette butts, even a pair of pink panties, left on the blood splattered sand.

A pair of thugs pushed him down the aisle and over to a large cage, where a small group of men were huddled, looking wet and wretched.

The gate was opened and he was thrust inside.

The group looked at him without much interest. Rook noticed that the two men nearest him were identical.

"Mods?" he asked.

"I'm David. That's Tad. Who're you?"

"Name's Rook Venner. How does this thing go?"

"You fight and then you die."

This mod had obviously had an upgrade, but Rook couldn't see an earback. The other men watching them had eyes bruised by recent experience. A couple of them were young white guys who looked terrified.

"And if I win?"

"Then they won't throw you to the gators." David pointed to a plank at the edge of the roof, then gestured to the giant screens. "They're in the water down below. They lens it, sell it on the 'net. Very popular in China, I heard."

"Gators?"

"Lots of them, and they're always hungry."

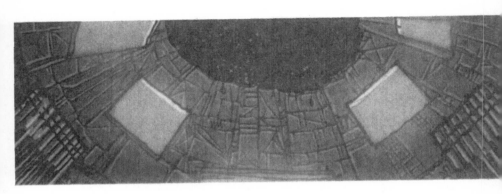

CHAPTER

Drums beat a steady cadence as the blood-red sun dipped below the horizon. Rook had spent the day in the cage, dazed by the heat.

Some vacation, he thought as he watched the fight come to a grisly end. Two closely matched men, both young, desperate, beat each other to a pulp.

"Real big shots." David sat with his back to the spectacle, leaning against the rusted iron bars of the fighters' cage. The mod was intelligent, but had no earback. "Whatever they owe Zato, they're paying now."

"Saves on interest." Rook's gaze flickered to the raised dais where Zato sat, surrounded by his goons. Food and booze

covered the tables before them. The leader's tacky suit had more sophistication than he did, but Zato ran his little kingdom well. Stay on his good side and you watched the entertainment; break his rules, and you were the entertainment.

One man had begun to fail. The other beat him to the floor and started kicking him, working vicious blows to the head.

The crowd started groaning and booing, bored, and the guards moved in, pulling the victor away and dragging the battered loser to his feet.

The announcer blared, "What say you? Give the loser what he deserves?"

"*Mátalo! Mátalo, ahora!*"

In the bleachers near Rook's cage, a group of young women screamed for the loser's blood, passing a jug of mescal around and laughing. Rook shivered; it was hard not to when confronted with people crying out for someone's death.

The announcer laughed menacingly. "*Adiós, amigo.*"

The guards dragged the loser onto the plank sticking out over the side of the building.

David glanced over his shoulder. "The lucky ones are dead before the gators get them."

Small mercy, thought Rook.

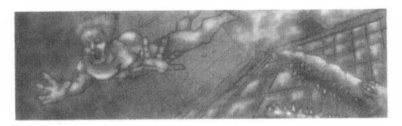

The guy was struggling, but the guards were used to that. The crowd went wild as the guards shoved the loser off the plank. For a moment he was almost flying, caught in the big lights, then he was gone, spiraling downward.

Everyone's attention turned to the virt screens suspended over the arena. Rook saw the guy hit the brightly lit water, lensed from multiple angles. The water suddenly came alive, churning with long, dark bodies. Then it

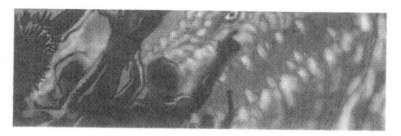

swirled deep red. People in the stands were on their feet, reveling in the brutal display.

Rook averted his eyes and thought about fighting instead. He'd always taken advantage of the training offered by the department, and it'd served him well in the uninsured world. Of course he'd never had to arrest an alligator.

A tall, lean, bronze-skinned man who'd been muttering to himself in the corner of the cage suddenly sprang at Rook.

"I hate this place!" he screamed.

"Okay." Rook cringed at the filthy man's rancid odor.

"You know what I hate even more?" he demanded.

"Mother's Day?"

"Cops! I kill you myself, motherfucker." The man leaned in close, wild eyes gleaming. "I kill you and fuck you when you're dead, before they throw you to the gators."

David pushed the guy away. "Save it for the ring, asshole."

"Shut your fuckin' mouth, you homo p-mod!"

David's eyes flashed cold steel. "You really want to make me mad?"

The guy snarled and moved away.

"Ignore Frito," David said. "He's crazier than the fucks out there."

Rook shrugged. On his list of mortal dangers, Frito ranked right below a mosquito bite.

"You been in here long?" Rook asked David.

"Few months."

"You must be a hell of a fighter."

"I survive."

The mod was a decent guy. Looking at the ragged assortment of crazies, mewling debtors, and homicidal maniacs crammed in the cage, Rook figured David was glad to have a sane conversation.

The guards came over to the cage. Rook tensed, tried to stay calm.

"Hey, Frito. You looking for action?" one of the guards snickered.

"I'll rip your guts out and feed them to your mother!" the man screamed.

"Keep it up, dickhead." The guards pulled Frito out and shoved him in the arena. The crowd hooted and roared, "Frito! Frito! Frito!" They knew what was coming. Evidently Frito was a favorite.

Another guard came from inside the buildings pushing a scared, blond teen ahead of them. The kid stumbled, fell, was pulled to his feet, slapped across the face, and shoved toward Frito.

"Jesus. That kid looks like he should be in school," said Rook.

"Just some fuckup didn't pay his cocaine bill," replied David.

Rook understood. Insured-world kids dabbling in drug dealing often fell afoul of more dangerous predators. He remembered finding the body of one James William Butler, nineteen, son of a wealthy Dutchess County lawyer. The kid had literally been crucified, nailed to a cross and left on the edge of a golf course in upper-crust Rivertown. Eventually some Crips were terminated in a night raid for that one.

"Don't be a dropout," announced Tad, who obviously hadn't had an upgrade like David.

The kid was no fighter, and Frito made short work of him, kicking him in the gut as he lay curled up like a big slug in the corner of the arena. The crowd started booing so the guards struck them with shock prods. That got the kid back on his feet.

It didn't last long. Frito moved in and started battering him with both hands. The kid couldn't fight, couldn't defend himself, and he was down and out cold inside two minutes.

Frito danced around the arena singing something made of madness and memory.

The kid was hauled out, to huge cheers from the crowd, then dragged across the roof and tossed to the gators down below.

The door to Rook's cage opened as Frito was shoved back inside.

The guard turned cold eyes to Rook and smiled a semi-toothless grin. "You." He motioned for Rook to step forward.

David held out his fist and knocked it against Rook's. "You know what to do, break something quickly."

Evidently, Rook was the main event tonight. Crowds filled the stands quickly as the announcer took the mic.

"Today, the great Zato brings you an extra special event. A policeman from New York!"

Zato stood and graced the crowd by chugging an entire bottle of tequila. He yelled and threw the bottle to the ground, smashing it to shards.

The crowd erupted in cheers and whistles, tossing beer cans and bottles in the air as the guards shoved Rook out of the cage and slammed the gate behind him.

"Taking on the policeman . . ." The announcer paused, waiting while the crowd screamed their favorites. "The Beast!"

The crowd roared its approval.

Below Zato's dais, steel doors swung open in front of Rook. A huge man walked into the fighting arena with a steady, unhurried tread. The man's long, scraggly hair framed a red slash pulling the right edge of his mouth into a permanent sneer. Tribal tattoos slashed with scars ran over his huge muscles. This guy was a nightmare on size-sixteen feet. The Beast stared at Rook, death in his cold, gray eyes.

Rook felt a shiver pass down his spine; he would be fighting for his life.

Thousands of eyes were all locked on Rook, eager for his death. He felt like a pig at a barbecue.

The crowd began a rhythmic chant:

"Mata la policía!"

Great, he thought. Kill the cop.

Rook and the Beast walked the ring, ten feet apart, sizing each other up. Rook observed on the giant the hallmarks of years of fighting. More than that, the man knew every inch of the arena; this was his home turf.

Rook took a deep breath, settled his weight on his heels, and did his best to ignore his obvious disadvantage.

The Beast came on fast, leading with a crisp left jab, then alternating with a sharp right.

Rook dodged, blocked, but the Beast brought in a hook, an uppercut, then a sudden leg sweep that almost caught Rook by surprise.

Rook danced away, snapping out his own left jab to keep the other man at bay.

They came together. Blows cracked off arms, elbows, palms. Rook's attempt with the right knee was blocked, but his counter with the left foot scored and the Beast grunted and moved out of range.

He came back fast. A crushing left uppercut to the ribs slammed Rook into the back wall.

The crowd surged to its feet, roaring in an ecstasy of bloodlust.

Rook's breath was gone, there was red in his vision. Another kick was coming, but he smothered it, got his arm around the leg. The Beast hit him again and again on the head with both fists. Rook got his legs under him and pushed off with everything he could muster. The Beast went backward, losing balance, and Rook kept the leg in his grip and toppled the bigger man onto his back.

Rook chanced a quick glance at David. The mod was pointing to his knee, yelling something. David knew the giant's weak point.

But the Beast had a perfectly trained rollout that took him out of range and brought him back smoothly to his feet and ready once again.

Tremors rocked through Rook's leaden legs. Blood was running down the side of his head. He was suddenly aware that this was how he was going to die. Beaten slowly to death by a monster in human form.

The Beast advanced, laughing like a rusty chain saw. Rook

put all the energy he could afford into his jab, trying to keep the bigger man away. They swapped kicks, then the Beast pivoted and drove in, ignored the jab, and grappled again.

The Beast held him with the right hand and punched with the left. Rook took a shot to the side of the head, saw stars, heard bells, blocked a knee aimed at his crotch, took another shot, punched back, but missed, and was carried back against the wall.

The big man's sneer wobbled in Rook's vision.

The Beast closed in, scenting the end now, sure of victory. Rook moved like a wounded animal, desperate, exhausted, beaten. The Beast had seen it many times before.

The crowd was jumping up and down, roaring, "Kill him! *Mátalo! Mátalo, ahora! Mata la policía!*"

Blows rained over his arms and shoulders. Sooner or later something would get through. He had to make his move now.

Rook got a knee up, blocking a kick, and that knocked both of them off-balance, but Rook didn't move, because

he couldn't. His legs were dead, and out of that came a miracle. Because as he went backward, the Beast had his right arm up, trying to keep his balance. A careless moment, an opportunity. Rook caught the trailing hand with a frantic grab and spun with it in his grip, putting everything into it. He turned it over, hard, pulled the Beast down, and dropped his full weight on the elbow joint.

Even over the noise of the crowd, Rook heard bones crack. He rolled clear, then got to his feet, unsteady, but alive.

The Beast was down to one arm.

The fight was over. The Beast circled away, aware that he was finished for the evening. He had a new look in those deadly eyes, fear.

Rook spat the blood welling in his mouth and turned his back on the Beast. He was done with this.

The crowd groaned, then roared their anger. Beer cans splattered on the bloody arena floor.

Rook ignored them all and stared across the heaving throng at Zato. Rook pointed at the grinning thug and cocked his finger like a gun.

"Mata el coño!" howled the mob.

Unable to sense his legs beneath him, Rook walked back to the cage. The door was opened, he went inside, heard the door slam behind him, and felt the ground rushing up toward him while everything seemed to spin. There was blackness, and silence, and other things that he knew nothing about.

CHAPTER

Mistress Julia could handle anything when it came to sex. Sex was her trade. She'd seen it all, every perversion known to man and some that weren't. So when Rico took her to his room, clumsily ripping her clothes off, she knew he was an amateur.

When the boy realized he couldn't toss her over his smelly bedclothes like a little play toy, he resorted to just ramming it into her.

But Mistress Julia was used to being in control. The dominatrix personality demanded obedience, and Rico, fingers digging into her hips, taking her from behind, needed a lesson in rules. Fortunately he was experienced enough

to have taken the trouble to lube things up, but there was still enough pain and degradation to focus her thoughts firmly on one thing: revenge. As sure as shit, that would come.

She didn't know what had happened to the cop and the pleasure mod. By herself, chances of escape were slim to none. But Rook and the upgraded mod had got them out of tough situations before. If they were still alive, she needed to find them. Her bank account was flush thanks to a grateful President Marion, who fortunately paid in advance. But if she ever wanted to spend it or see her house in upstate New York again, she had to find the mod. This little shit had no idea whom he was dealing with.

Already, Rico had become addicted to having her take him into her mouth. She'd demonstrated such fantastic skills, the boy would never be able to get enough.

When he'd first dragged her into this dark cave of a bedroom, she'd been aware that he didn't have high hopes. He'd told her that she better fuck him good or he'd beat

her senseless and put her out to screw passersby for small change.

That had passed with one blow job. When a girl stuck her head in the door and called his name, he'd sworn at her, saying he was with his new woman now and to take a hike.

Julia smiled. That's right, I'm your woman now. It was pay or play, and Mistress Julia told the small, frightened voice deep in her head to just shut up and let her play. The mistress was going to get in this motherfucker's head, and then, oh, baby, there was gonna be some *real* fucking. The payback kind.

* * *

The next day the sun beat down on the cage without mercy.

"I wiped the crust off." David handed Rook a ladle of murky liquid. "It won't kill you."

Rook gratefully drank some of the brackish water. Every time he moved, an orchestra of aches and pains reminded him of the night before.

David had cleaned Rook up and applied crude bandages to the cuts on his shoulder.

"Thanks," Rook said, handing the ladle back. He pulled himself to his feet, tried stretching, and groaned as souvenirs from the Beast informed him of their condition.

"Got to try and stay limber," said David. "You made quite an impression. They're gonna want to see you fight again."

"Regular three-ring circus."

"Eat this. As fresh as it gets." David handed Rook a plate of beans with grisly-looking fried plantains and cornmeal.

Rook wolfed it down, grease and unsalted mush hitting his bruised, empty stomach like cement in a balloon.

"The Beast has been here for years." David sat down next to Rook. "He's never lost."

"I don't doubt that."

Rook ran a hand over the left side of his face. He was a mess, but the wounds had scabbed over, and the bandages had helped stop the blood flow. He was going to have some heavy scars. Not to worry. He was more likely to be dead than ugly.

In the distance, Rook could see that the river had claimed a wide swath of territory to the west and north of the tower blocks. Rain had swollen the streams, and he caught the silvery glint of water stretching to the horizon.

Farther west there seemed to be forest; the east was a jagged landscape of abandoned buildings. And somewhere in the distance, a thin line of fence marked off insured territory from this wasteland. As a cop, Rook had always been conscious of the law of the jungle that ruled here, a tumor in the body of American civilization. Just a few miles away, people were getting lattes and pizza, going home for hot virt sex. But here, on this side of the fence, insured civilization seemed like nothing more than a dream.

Rook tried to relax, leaning back against the wall of the cage as David tied off another bandage. David's friend, Tad, sat next to him. Their conversation started with the fights, which took place most nights, and were the major

social event in the life of the former Simms-Canton housing project.

"How you come here?" asked Tad.

"Long story." Rook sighed. He had time to kill. "I was a homicide detective assigned to protect a witness and wound up here instead."

Tad laughed. "You not very good policeman."

"I fucked up."

Which was, unfortunately, the truth.

David seemed interested. "What happened to the witness?"

"She's here. Inside somewhere, helpless. Her name is Plesur."

"Plesur? That's a . . ."

"Yeah."

"You risked your life for a mod?" David's eye shone with surprise, almost gratitude.

"It's a living." Rook shrugged. "How'd you end up here?"

David wiped a trickle of sweat from his brow. Like all

Davids, he was lean-jawed, handsome, with level blue eyes, corn-blond hair, even teeth, very white.

"I belonged to a guy in New York City, Vincent. He worked insurance. Told me he loved me. Bought me the upgrade."

"I don't see an earback."

"I had the Campbell-Ritter surgery." Off Rook's confused look, David explained, "They grow extra brain cells, filter them into the areas that are deficient in the basic model. Takes a lot longer, and it costs a lot more."

"Fairy-tale romance."

David grinned. "Without the happy ending."

"What happened?"

"Vincent liked to share me. His hobby was photography. One day, he just didn't come home. I didn't know too much then. I was learning from TV and virt. Then his sister came and sold me to a fight club. They trained me to fight the circuit."

Rook shook his head. "Rough road to travel."

"Everyone likes to see someone die in the ring."

People were hard to understand sometimes. Rook had grown a callus over that part of his mind. You had to in his work. Over the years he'd seen just about everything. A mother hanged by her twin twelve-year-old sons in her own kitchen. A boy burned to death by his father, who was convinced the kid was the son of Satan. Killings of every kind and level of brutality. You had to concentrate on just doing the job, and not think too much about how sick human beings could be.

"I'm no fight whore!" David said angrily, then relaxed. "Some of the other mods and I escaped. We were living not far from here until Zato's boys grabbed us."

Rook noted David's composure. To be treated as somewhere between a slave and a dog, a house pet for sexual services, it had to be hard to look back on.

"Other guys still around?"

David shook his head. "Except Tad. He doesn't have an upgrade so I look out for him."

"You're a good man. Not right to be locked in here like an animal."

David smiled gratefully.

Rook sat back under the broiling sun, consciously conserving energy, and wondering where Plesur was. At least he knew no one would touch her until someone came to pick her up. But who? Did Sable Ranch deal with the

likes of Zato, or was someone else after her? He had until then to figure out how the hell to get out of this fuckup.

When the sun had set in a riot of color in the west, the fans started pouring in, filling the stands for another night of brutality. Guards lit torches around the ring with flamethrowers. Rook had the uneasy feeling his odds of seeing tomorrow night were getting slimmer by the minute.

A group of women sauntered over to the cage to check out the policeman.

"Yo! Police, you sexy motherfucker!" A leering chola ground her body suggestively against the bars, flashing silver canine teeth and emerald studs set into her eyebrows. "Gonna watch you dance tonight!"

Another one, wearing nothing but flimsy-looking green lace over her huge tits, called out, "Everyone betting on you tonight."

Rook knew better than to respond.

"Policeman, you win, I let you kiss my pussy."

Rook grinned at her. "Sorry, I'm on duty."

It took a few seconds for the joke to penetrate, but then she laughed.

"*Bueno, ése.* You funny. When you die, we laugh, okay?"

"Knock yourself out." Rook turned away from her, studied the rooftop in the fading sunset.

The lights were switched on as soon as it grew dark. Drums started beating, sending out a slow, steady throb.

Rook had dozed off when someone rapped the bars by his head. Jarred from his nap, Rook turned to see Zato, gleaming scars caught in the light.

"You a good fighter, Detective Venner."

"Let her go before it's too late."

Zato laughed, silver teeth flashing. He handed Rook a bottle through the bars. "Go ahead, good tequila."

Frito ran over, practically salivating as Rook took a deep swig. He handed the bottle to David.

Zato leaned in close to Rook. "You like mods, eh?"

"Just one."

"She is *muy importante.*"

Rook stared back, saying nothing.

"You know, Detective, you lose one opportunity, you find another," Zato sneered.

The guards entered the cage and pushed David to his feet beside Rook.

"You like mods so much, you die with one." The gang leader sauntered back to the stands.

Rook's stomach lurched as the guards clamped one cold iron cuff around Rook's right ankle and secured the other on David's left ankle, chaining them together.

They were handed bloodstained leather gloves with metal studs.

"Tag team," said David grimly. "We're tied together, but the ones we fight will be free."

Rook tested the gloves. They were tight and had limited padding, but they were also heavy. "We'll see who lives and who dies tonight."

CHAPTER 7

Mistress Julia had trained all her life for this moment.

"*Pobrecito,*" she whispered as she mothered Rico with her truly magnificent breasts. "You're so much better than all of them."

Mistress Julia rode Rico skillfully, bringing him close to a climax and then stopping, leaving him shuddering and panting, balanced on the edge of losing control, then slowly sliding back down into the pool of dark desires.

Once she had the key, Mistress Julia soon unlocked Rico, that little boy inside the hulk of muscle and metal. Things had been difficult for him. Zato's younger cousin, Rico was always lost in the shadow of his famous relative. Constantly pushed to see how tough he really was, he fought plenty when he was just one of the kids running around on the plazas.

"*Sí,*" he whispered. "They will all soon know."

Rico felt underappreciated by Zato and the other top honchos.

"One day soon they'll see how smart you are," she cooed in his ear. "You were smart enough to get me."

"So much woman."

She held him close, let him suckle her perfect nipples, let the smooth, round flesh of her breasts bounce softly against the tormented skin of his face, transforming his usual momentary pleasure into a prolonged surf along the curl of ecstasy, until he was slowly, but carefully, turned inside out.

"You know what makes a real man?" she breathed.

Rico pressed himself against her, eager, ready. "I'll show you."

"It's having a real woman by your side," she murmured.

"Someone who knows how strong you are. The others respect you because they want her."

"You are my woman now."

"No one else can have me because I belong to you," she breathed, holding him back from climax.

Mistress Julia was damn good. It had always impressed Angie whenever she stood back and watched the Julia personality at work. On her own she would have been terrified. But that was the point of the Julia chip, it freed Angie from herself. It was time to set the bait.

"I know how to make your cock so hard, your head will explode."

Rico moaned, eager to experience these new heights of ecstasy.

"We should bring someone else to the party, another girl," she said, rubbing herself against his thigh. Like an actress trained to cry on cue, Julia could make herself wet.

"Nobody as good as you, *mija*."

"There is one. A pleasure model."

Rico stopped abruptly, and for a second Julia thought she had gone too far. "Zato's prisoner," he said. "The Overlords are coming for her."

Julia shrugged, drawing his attention back to her breasts. "Exactly, she'll be gone soon enough, and a stupid mod would say nothing. I'll enjoy it, but you, you have never experienced anything like that, trust me. Come on, Rico, let's have some fun."

Rico was uncertain, but hard-ons didn't lie. Eyes full of lust, he used his second brain to make a decision. "Everyone is at the fights. She's alone in one of Zato's apartments. I have the key."

Julia lovingly caressed him. "Lead the way, lover."

Up on the roof, it was a different game. The drums thundered, whistles blew, and the crowd chanted, "Death to the police," as the bloodred sun dripped in the western sky.

"You like to dance?" Rook moved awkwardly, trying to gauge his mobility.

David smirked. "I'm the life of the party."

"Try to stay in step with me."

They could hardly maneuver, chained together with a four-foot length of steel chain. If either of them moved too sharply, he could pull the other's leg out from under him and drag them both down.

Their opponents were a pair of young wannabe gangers, barely out of their teens, trying to make a name by killing the police and the homo p-mod. A big opportunity for these punks, and they'd dressed for the occasion. Their skin glistened with oil, the steel implants in their faces polished and shining. One of them had his hair pulled back in a ponytail. The other's shaved head was a canvas of dark tattoos. Their eyes glittered.

Rook adjusted his studded leather gloves, eyeing the five-foot-long bamboo poles that the young thugs carried. With Rook and David unable to move far or fast, their opponents could strike at will. Rook and David stood with their backs to the wall.

"Shall we?" Rook met David's cool gaze.

"You lead."

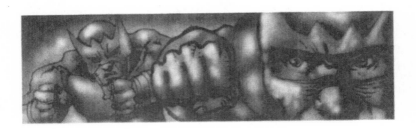

Their opponents circled, then pushed forward, lashing at them, then jumping back. Using the glove, Rook deflected the blows easily enough.

"Try to lure them in, bring them close," Rook instructed.

David understood. If they could get hold of one of the bamboo poles, or if one of the thugs came in range, they had a shot.

The youths realized after a few minutes that this wasn't working and switched tactics. Now both converged on Rook. He tried to ward off the blows, but he couldn't stop them all, collecting shots to the head, cheeks, and legs. David reached in and tried to deflect the onslaught.

That caused the punks to switch to him, and the mod was forced back to the wall. Rook scrambled after him, feeling the cuff pull dangerously tight against his ankle.

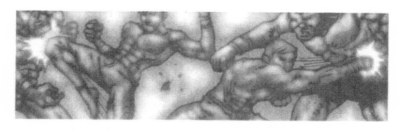

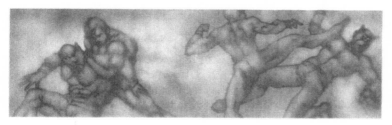

He had barely regained his balance when the bamboo lashed his head and shoulders. Rook concentrated on trying to grab it, but the other cane cracked down on his knuckles.

Suddenly someone else leaped into the ring. Rook froze as a bizarre man in some kind of tribal headdress pranced around them. The headpiece lit up with hundreds of miniature lights like a UFO on steroids. The man screamed viciously.

"Oh, shit," Rook heard David mutter.

The youths pulled back, smiling and laughing.

"Who's the Christmas tree?" said Rook, wiping sweat off his face.

"Cuatomoc," David spat. "Zato's favorite psycho."

In one huge fist, Cuatomoc clutched an iron rod crackling with electric sparks. One jolt from that on the chain connecting David and Rook, and they were toast. Cuatomoc stalked the perimeter of the arena, eyes glazed with bloodlust, waiting for the opportunity to strike.

"You gonna fry, *marrano*." The bald kid whipped his cane through the air, catching Rook behind the knee. David lurched forward as Rook stumbled.

With a maniacal shriek, Cuatomoc struck hard with the iron prod.

Rook dodged the blow, and the rod jammed into the ground, releasing an explosion of sparks.

"Light my fire, fucker." Rook pounded the man's side, followed by a roundhouse smack into his chin. The headdress lit up like the Fourth of July.

The crowd whistled and roared approval. This was more like it.

Cuatomoc pulled free and spun away, snarling. The punks rammed into David again and again while Cuatomoc leveled his weapon at Rook.

Women began baying like hounds as blood flew off David's head and shoulders.

Cuatomoc whipped the iron bar low and hard. Rook jerked his left leg aside, dragging the chain away, but paid with an electric shock just above the ankle.

It hurt like a motherfucker.

Rook tried to gain his footing, but half his leg had gone numb. "Shit!"

Cuatomoc reversed and came in the other way. Rook dodged a blow to the head, but it pulled him sideways on his dead leg, too far away from David.

"Stay close to me!" Rook ordered.

Cuatomoc struck wildly, scoring a hard shot to David's waist, trailing sparks over the mod's left side. David wobbled. One of the punks hit him across the head, sending blood splattering across the ground. Then, to Rook's horror, David slipped backward and went down.

"Muy bonita, ése!"

Rico was all smiles, strutting like a rooster past the admiring girls and guys in the hallway.

Julia held her head high, daring anyone to try to fuck with her man. She was careful to lean into the arm Rico wrapped possessively around her waist.

The roar of the crowd filtered through the open windows.

"Big fight tonight," she breathed.

"They got a policeman in the cage. Tough motherfucker. Gonna take some time to put him down." Rico winked.

Julia winced. There was no time left. She had to play this perfectly, the best game of her career. Rico took the stairwell down a level and entered a dimly lit hallway. The deep-pile carpet helped make their passage silent. They slunk past three women gossiping in a kitchen, the smell of acrid spices thick in the air as they made their way to the door at the end of the corridor.

Rico took a key from his pocket, a Valuz, very high end, deceptively simple looking. "This is the place of dreams, *corazón.*"

Julia moved close beside Rico, resting her hands on his hip and stroking his hard, young muscles. "You make me so fucking horny. Hurry, baby."

The key slipped into the little slot in the door. After a moment of protocol adjustment the door opened.

Zato had knocked down the walls of four rooms, making one huge vault.

"Someday this will be all mine."

Rico hit a switch and light bathed the room. Stacks and stacks of cash, cocaine bricks, and masses of electronics were piled up against the walls.

"Check it out." Rico ran his hands over the loot, performing like a little boy showing off to a girl he wanted to impress.

"What's in this?" Julia ran her hand over a slick steel door.

Rico hit a button and the wall opened to reveal a well lit walk-in closet. Julia tried to contain her triumphant smile. Jackpot. Racks of rifles, boxes of grenades, and tac-armor hung on the wall. But what caught her eye sat on a tabletop flashing a small red light; Rook Venner's fancy phone, his gun, and glittering like jewels—the combat earbacks from ex-president Marion's place.

"Where is she?" Julia asked, keeping her voice soft and husky as she turned Rico around.

"The bedroom." Rico squeezed Julia's firm ass. "You are so much woman," he whispered. "How much more can the mod be?"

"You have no idea," she enticed him, as they moved toward the bedroom door.

Rico swung the door open, splashing ragged light across the bed. Plesur sat up, staring at them blankly.

Julia kissed Rico hard before moving to the bed.

"Qué deliciosa." Rico was practically delirious with lust as he began stripping off his clothes.

Julia sat by Plesur and gently took the mod's head in her hands, brushing her lustrous blond hair behind her ears.

"I know you?" Plesur asked, blue eyes wide with anticipation.

"I'm your friend," Julia whispered quickly. "Are you okay?"

"Everything is bad."

"Maybe this will help, sweetie."

Julia slid the earback from her pocket and inserted it in the stud behind the mod's ear.

* * *

"Get up!" Rook snarled, standing over David's body.

Rook was a tapestry of cuts, his blood running in dark rivers to the sand. But he refused to go easily. He would die slowly, he would die hard. He would never give up.

Bamboo slashed his face. He flinched, grabbed at it, but missed. Cuatomoc swung in with the iron rod. Rook ducked as it crackled over his head.

"Get the fuck up!"

There was a groan and David moved.

Cuatomoc jumped forward and tried to hammer the mod. Rook deflected the blow, and for a moment he had his fingers around the rod, but slicked with blood, it slipped easily from his grasp. Shock waves ran up his arm. Fire glinted as metal came hurtling down.

David's body slammed the lunatic warrior, throwing him to the ground.

"Thanks." Rook tried to flex his tingling fingers, couldn't.

"No problemo," David rasped, wobbly but standing.

Cuatomoc had a savage smile now, knowing that victory was close. "Wake up, it's time to fry."

Roaring, he attacked, and Rook took a shot to his midriff, driving the air out of his body. Cuatomoc roared in triumph and closed in, driving Rook back into the wall of the cage and bringing the iron rod high overhead for the death stroke.

In desperation, Rook dropped to his right knee and swung his left leg in a sweep at ankle height.

Cuatomoc hadn't expected that and it caught him. He went up in the air and fell crashing to the ground.

Rook flung himself forward on top of Cuatomoc. David followed, ignoring the blows from the bamboo, pinning Cuatomoc between them.

Rook punched in the headdress with his numb right hand and saw the lights go out. David grabbed Cuatomoc's head and snapped his neck.

When they stood up, Rook brandished the iron bar in his left hand. The boys with the bamboo backed away.

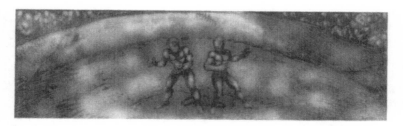

The ringing in Rook's ears grew to an ocean roar but it wasn't the crowd. It was the sound of an engine screaming over the roof.

CHAPTER

The night sky brightened as a heavy thrumming noise swept over the building. A sleek black helicopter was descending toward the roof.

It came down smoothly, settling with hardly a bump. Rook saw it wasn't military or police, but a corporate luxury transport, not what you would expect around these parts.

The door popped open and a trio of massive men got out. They had expensive-looking suits, immaculately coiffed hair, and mirrorshade wraparounds. They were all the same height and physique, square, blocky. The only way of telling them apart was the slight variations on their creamy white suits and paisley shirts.

The way they moved, almost machinelike, gorilla muscles bulging under the expensive silk suits, they were mechanically enhanced like Skelsa and his FBI crew.

The crowd fell eerily silent.

"Overlords," said David.

"Just when you think you've seen it all."

The Overlords were supposed to be an urban myth, an elite, all-powerful crime syndicate. Rook had heard plenty of stories. Some claimed they splintered from Yakuza, others said Russian mob. Didn't matter. They were real, and Rook had the sinking feeling he knew why they had come.

David watched the Overlords stride toward Zato. "Wonder what dragged them down from Mount Olympus."

Rook tensed. "They're here for Plesur."

The bio giants were met by Zato and his top guys. Rook observed that Zato had suddenly become humble, bowing and showing off his *casa*.

Then with a wave of a hand, he led them into the ring.

"Detective," said Zato. "You are honored, some very important people want you dead."

The Overlords' array of N$15,000 suits, the N$10,000 boots, the little diamond-studded accoutrements, made a startling contrast to the ugly spikes sticking out of Zato and his boys.

"SIO Venner," said one of them. "You look like shit." The accent was close to neutral.

Rook stared at the row of mirrorshades, then smiled, aware that he was covered in blood, cuts, and bruises, his clothes in tatters. "I've had worse days."

The trio smiled, revealing perfect white teeth.

"Lot of muscle for one little pleasure mod," said Rook, stepping closer. "You know I'm going to kill you."

The Overlords laughed, as well as Zato and his henchmen.

"You going to come over here and do it yourself?" one Overlord mocked.

"Don't have to."

That confused them. The Overlords exchanged a look. "You are crazy, even for a cop."

"Operation Taste Imperative."

"That means nothing."

"Now you know." Rook grinned. "Soon as they find out you know, good-bye nice suit."

The trio drew back with a collective snarl.

One of them reached into his jacket and pulled out a massive, gleaming handgun. "I would kill you like a dog, but Zato has better plans."

A squad of heavies quickly dragged Cuatomoc's body away. The two young thugs had disappeared. The crowd murmured as a nervous guard removed the chain from Rook's and David's legs.

Rook stood unflinching, refusing to acknowledge the deep gash from the iron cuff, his bleeding palms, loose tooth, the welts and bruises throbbing all over his body.

David held himself together, too, standing up as straight as his battered, bleeding body would let him. The only emotion visible on his grotesquely swelling face was pride. Nobody was going to beat him down.

Rook squared his shoulders.

"You got something going on with these pleasure mods." Zato suddenly lashed out and slapped David hard across the face. David didn't move, but his eyes glowed with hate.

Rook said nothing, just kept his thousand-yard stare flat and level.

"You like this *puto* so much?" said Zato playing to the crowd. "I give you both the chance to live. You fight each other now."

"I won't do it."

"You win, you live to fight another day. The loser, well, he loses." Zato raised his arms and the crowd cheered.

The guard tossed a pair of wicked knives at Rook's and David's feet.

"Go fuck yourselves," Rook growled.

"Kill this motherfucker," one of the Overlords instructed David. "I'll make sure you get out of here alive."

David listened without any reaction.

Zato had a weird little grin on his face as he escorted the gangster executives to the dais.

The guard waved his automatic rifle at the knives. "Pick them up, scumbags."

Feeling incredibly weary, Rook obeyed, threw one to David.

"Sorry it had to end this way," said David.

"Yeah."

The guard sprayed bullets over their heads. "Fight, or we break your arms and throw you both off the roof."

Rook dropped into a fighting crouch, holding the knife in his left hand. It was an old trick, and it confused David, who kept looking at the knife with obvious questions running through his mind.

Rook feinted with the blade, they closed, and David slashed at him. The mod was strong, but he and Rook were tired from the previous fight.

David came closer and whispered, "You have to save her. If these guys want her, she's important."

They stumbled together, almost fell.

Rook took what he hoped would be a convincing jab with the knife, expecting David to dodge left. But David left his neck exposed, and the blade grazed his jugular, leaving a bright red line.

"What are you doing?" Rook demanded.

"I'm a mod. I don't have many years left."

Realization filled Rook's swollen eyes, he lowered his knife. "I won't do it."

"Only one of us is walking out of here." David shoved Rook away. "Fight, you fucking coward police!" he shouted, sending the crowd into fits of laughter and whistling.

David slashed again and the tip of his knife cut across Rook's chest. Rook felt it slicing his flesh, hot blood running down his chest. He staggered into the rear wall and went down on one knee.

The Overlords watched impassively.

Rook struggled to get back on his feet.

"I've seen a lot, done a lot. More than most mods can say." David's eyes were full of compassion.

The crowd was on its feet, howling for death to the "policeman."

"You're a cop. You have a chance to do something important." David circled, spreading his arms wide, an easy target for a direct strike. "Come on, do it!"

Mistress Julia ran a quick check of the items she'd liberated. The gun, a Chancellor 7.62 machine pistol with four

clips, each with twenty rounds; a sheath knife with a razor-sharp eight-inch blade that she'd strapped to her right thigh and various grenades.

All this stuff went into the neat little black backpack she'd found in a corner.

"Take those, too," she told Plesur, who was now armed to the teeth, loading ammunition into spare clips for the rifle she'd removed from the rack.

Outside they could hear the crowd roaring. Must be one hell of a fight.

Julia handed Plesur a knife, and another gun. "Clock's ticking, baby girl."

Plesur practically glowed as intelligence flooded her eyes. "Motherfuckers will pay." She locked and loaded.

Julia grinned. "Looks like I picked the right earback."

"What about him?" Plesur nodded to the miserable figure on the bed trussed up like a pig to slaughter.

"I think he'll be all right, won't you, *corazón?*"

Rico was gagged, tied down over a stack of cocaine bricks in the "offering" position that Mistress Julia used with her

most submissive clients. His wrists were bound to his ankles and his ass was stuck up in the air. He groaned and struggled to no avail. Mistress Julia knew everything there was to know about tying someone up, and how to keep him that way. But what horrified Rico was the piece of wire stuck halfway down a lit candle. When the flame reached it, the coil would superheat—and the other end was shoved about two inches up his rectum.

"You're lucky I didn't kill you," she told the whimpering Rico. "Oh, and by the way? Zato was wrong. You're even more stupid than he thinks."

She opened the door to the hallway. "You ready?"

Plesur nodded, ready for a killer time.

CHAPTER 9

"Fight!" snarled the guard, firing the gun over the rooftop.

The crowd responded by firing their own weapons into the air. The drums pounded a steady cadence.

Zato sat on the dais with his guests, who ignored the women laying out trays of food and cocaine. He wasn't even paying attention to the fight anymore, so wrapped up was he in making a good impression on the Overlords.

"Don't make it any worse." David wiped a rivulet of blood from his eye.

"That would be difficult."

Rook and David circled, knives held low. Rook didn't know how long he could stay standing, his leg was bad and the rest of him no better. His mind spun, trying to figure another way out of this, something that would save both their lives. Delay too long, and they'd both be thrown to the gators; the Overlords would take Plesur, her secrets extracted, her life forfeit. But nobody deserved to die in this ring, and Rook had never liked being the hatchet man.

David swung in, slashed at him. Rook saw it coming and blocked it easily. He parried another slash and tried to hook David's knife arm for a hold. David wriggled away and came back strong.

"Are you always so stubborn?" the mod asked.

"Regular rock."

They closed, slashed, blocked. David evaded the first thrust, but Rook spun, hit him with a right elbow, and followed with a leg sweep that took the mod's right leg clean out from under him. David fell, awkwardly, started to roll, then Rook came down on him, trying to pin him, not stab him. David pushed up, got an arm free. They were each holding the other's knife hand, so it was just a test of strength.

Rook climbed back to his feet. "I won't kill you."

David, along with everyone else, had to have seen that. The policeman hadn't killed the mod when he could have.

The crowd did not appreciate mercy, especially in this case.

A powerful electric shock shot through the back of Rook's right leg like fire.

A glance behind showed the guard grinning at him. "You want some more?"

Rook stumbled, the leg was gone, he couldn't feel a thing, and it wouldn't support him.

The guard zapped him again, this time on the hip, and Rook fell to the ground.

The crowd liked that, the roar that went up was deafening.

The guard raised his arms and bellowed, eager to please the spectators.

"They won't stop until one of us is dead." David crawled over, plainly worried. He might not even need to finish the job.

They grappled, Rook felt his right leg giving way. He was forced to hang on to David's shoulder, opening his own rib cage to the knife.

"You gonna kill him or kiss him?" the guard mocked. The crowd roared with laughter. The guard laughed along with them, broken teeth turned to the bleachers.

"I got a better idea." David heaved Rook out of the way and leaped to his feet.

The guard's laughter abruptly drowned in a gurgle of blood as the knife drove through his neck.

The crowd leaped to their feet, straining to see what

had happened. Caught in the harsh glare of the lights, all they saw was blood gushing to the sand. Then the guard fell back, grasping at the knife stuck in his throat, blood fountaining up from the sliced artery.

The world flashed white.

It was as if someone had hit the mute button. Rook couldn't even hear his breathing as he slid down on his left knee.

David was yelling something, but Rook only saw the mod's lips moving. Smoke filled the rooftop as people ran for cover, firing weapons and trying to figure out who or what had dared to assault their lair.

David reached down and hoisted Rook to his feet.

Smoke curled over the ring, obscuring the view. A figure like some crazy Japanese shadow dancer was making its way toward Rook and David. The shadow spun and fired, kicking bodies out of its way. Anyone who tried to stop it was leveled, until nobody stood in its path.

Rook had barely taken in this hallucination when a second deafening explosion ripped the night in two.

"What the fuck?" David shouted.

Rook swallowed. At least his hearing wasn't permanently damaged.

Silhouetted by smoke, a woman stood, gun raised and ready. Plesur stepped forward, holding an assault rifle.

"Plesur." Shock and relief battled it out on Rook's face.

"I missed you, too." Plesur swung the rifle over one shoulder and draped Rook's arm over the other. David limped to Rook's other side.

Plesur eyed the other mod curiously.

"Your helpless mod I presume." David smiled.

"Plesur, David. David, Plesur."

The mods nodded at one another, moving Rook quickly out of the arena.

The roof was pandemonium, spectators stampeding to the exits amid smoke, flames, and gunfire. A guard charged at them, flipping the safety off his semiautomatic. Plesur took him out with a kick to his groin without so much as breaking stride. David bent over the downed guard and snatched a set of keys.

"You got an army with you?" asked David.

A tall woman dressed in black leather materialized from the smoky chaos. "That would be me."

David took in the arsenal strapped to the domme. "Whoa."

Julia gave Rook's bruises a critical look. "You okay?"

"Terrific."

"Figured you'd want these." She handed him his sidearm and the Nokia.

The phone buzzed happily in his hand, indicating she was safe and functional. "Reunited with all my girls."

The prisoners were piled on top of one another along the cage walls, screaming.

"We need to take that chopper!" Rook ordered. "Let's go now!"

"We can't leave yet!" David had run the other way,

unlocking the cage. Prisoners flew out, charging into the fray, eager to get their hands on their captors.

Julia pulled a grenade from her bag, switched it on, and tossed it into the crowd. Rook saw the muzzle flashes, but didn't hear anything because the sonic had just ripped everyone's eardrums left to right.

"God, I love these things!" Julia exulted. "What are they?"

"Sonic grenades," Rook shouted. The chopper stood not ten yards away, lights flashing like a bright toy. "David, come on!"

The mod reappeared, guiding someone toward them. It was Tad, looking upset and scared.

"It's okay, Tad. Don't be afraid," David soothed his friend.

"Shit." Rook's plan evaporated with the sound of heavy rotors whining as thrusters ignited.

The helicopter burst from the roof, ascending into the night sky.

"Hellava rescue," Rook told Julia. "Now what?"

The domme raised another sonic grenade. "I have a few more of these, unless you have a better plan."

Plesur had been scanning the roof, her eyes settling on a steady stream of fighters running toward the ramp overhanging the building. "We have to jump."

"That wasn't it," Julia said.

But Rook knew Plesur was right. "The crowd would tear us apart before we got to the stairs. There's no other way out."

"Fuck." Julia put the grenade back in her pack. "Don't have an earback that makes you fly, do you?"

"David take Tad home now?" Tad asked, eyes wide with worry.

"Yes, Tad. We go home now."

Mods, domme, and cop fought their way through the mayhem, stopping near the plank.

A prisoner spun around and fell off the roof, shot through the head, tumbling down into the night.

Rook looked over the edge. Ten stories straight down into a pool of horrors waiting for them in the water below. "Shoulda worn my swimming trunks."

David gripped Tad's shoulders. "We can make it."

"How deep you think it is?" Rook asked.

"With all the heavy rains, should be at least ten feet," David figured.

Rook turned to his friends. "Feetfirst when you hit the water. It's gonna hurt, but not as much as breaking your neck," he heard himself say, as if from far away. "When you surface, we stick together and make a straight shot to solid ground."

A bullet smacked into the concrete beside his foot. Plesur turned and emptied her clip into the madness. The mob was fighting to get through the doors and back down the stairs. All the prisoners ran free including an elated Frito, doing as much damage as he could.

But Zato's men were coming, lots of them, and they had plenty of guns.

"We can't wait," Plesur urged.

"Whatever you did," Rook said to Julia as they moved toward the edge of the roof, "thanks."

Julia looked his way and he was struck by how beautiful she was, her hair gone wild with the humidity and the big machine pistol in her hands.

"Piece of cake," she said with a grim little smile. "This is the hard part."

They lined up on the edge. It was a long way down.

More and more prisoners were jumping now, hitting the waters in a crescendo of screams.

"Tad, hold your breath," David instructed. "When we hit the water, we have to swim, okay?"

"Okay, David." Tad slipped his hand into his friend's.

"Plesur, I'm sorry for everything," Rook said. "I was supposed to protect you."

She smiled. "I'm still here."

"See you at the bottom." David and Tad jumped first, followed by Julia.

Rook took Plesur in his arms. "Whatever happens, we'll be together."

The look in her eyes said always.

They stepped off the edge into emptiness.

CHAPTER 10

Rook and Plesur hit the water together, feetfirst, but they still went down a good ways. Rook touched bottom, the surreal image of a former basketball court wavering in the brightly lit water. Grabbing Plesur, he kicked them both to the surface.

Screams, thrashing water, and confusion surrounded them.

He coughed, clearing water from his lungs. The impact had taken his breath away, but he was alive, at least for the moment.

Plesur sucked in ragged breaths, spitting water while trying to stay afloat.

"Hold on to me," he shouted. He caught a momentary flash of blue eyes, and she came into his arms, gripping him hard.

Heavy splashes crashed around them. Rook shielded Plesur from the rain of bodies, trying to avoid getting crushed.

"David!" he called out. "Julia!"

Harsh lights streamed over the water from the roof, but he couldn't see the mods or the domme. A crowd packed on a terrace midway up the building was practically dancing with excitement. Rook covered Plesur's head and dodged a volley of rocks pitched by laughing children.

Dark shapes surged through the water. Dozens of gators swarmed in a feeding frenzy, slicing through bright ribbons of blood floating on the surface.

A prisoner with a scarred face and terrified eyes grabbed desperately for Rook. As Rook tried to ward him off, a dark mass burst from the water. Long jaws seized the man with a quick shake of its massive head, dragging the shocked prisoner underwater.

Keeping Plesur's head above water, Rook fished his gun out of his pants. "David! Julia!"

With a huge splash right beside them, another tumbling body fell into the water.

Something solid and spiky brushed Rook's leg. Massive creatures were swimming around them, sensing fresh prey. Rook knew he couldn't outswim them, and fighting in deep water was suicide. He held Plesur to his chest, fired three shots at the monstrous shadows, and used a side stroke to pull them toward the concrete shore. The only chance they had was that the gators were so busy, they could slip through.

"Venner!"

Through the mass of thrashing arms and legs, he saw David making his way toward them. Tad trailed limply in his friend's arms. Looked as if the poor mod had broken his leg on impact.

"Head toward the shallows!" Rook shouted.

An immense shadow slithered behind the mods.

"Behind you!" Rook aimed his gun but could not fix the target.

The ten-foot-long monster lunged from the water and clamped its jaws on Tad.

Tad screamed as the alligator ripped into his torso. Blood sprayed into the air, clouding the water.

David was vainly trying to pull the alligator's jaws apart, but it was too late. Blood poured from Tad's mouth as the mod was pulled under.

"Tad!" David shouted.

Rook fired wild shots into the water as more gators slithered around them, attracted by fresh blood. David was completely surrounded.

Like an avenging angel, Julia rose from the water beside Rook and Plesur, pumping bullets into the monsters.

A path cleared and David swam toward them, face stricken with shock and grief.

"He's gone." Rook grabbed David's arm. "Let's go!"

Rook redoubled his efforts with the side stroke and was rewarded a few moments later with the touch of concrete to his fingertips.

He put a leg down, they were in the shallows.

Plesur followed his lead, steadying him as he tested his right leg. Still a bit numb, but it would hold his weight. Together they hoisted themselves onto the damp concrete and pulled themselves out of the gator pit.

"We made it," Plesur whispered. In the dim light, water dripped from her hair and trickled over her perfect body.

"We were lucky." Rook checked his pockets for the Nokia.

Ingrid had made it through the drop.

He turned back and saw Julia, gleaming in wet leather,

coming out of the water, holding the Chancellor machine pistol in her hand.

"You okay?" he said as he helped her out.

"Hit someone on the way into the water, I'm gonna have a bruise or two."

Rook looked behind her; saw David coming out of the water, alone. Long gashes raked his arms.

"Oh, shit." Julia grabbed the mod's arms and helped him onto the concrete. Her expert gaze surveyed his wounds. "He needs help."

Rook eyed a small gator, thrashing in the water, trying to climb ashore. He took a quick look around, searching for the best route out. The whole area had once been a complex of sunken playgrounds and high terraces. Now, the submerged playgrounds were home to the well-fed gators. By good fortune he'd chosen to swim into what had been a landing, an upper tier to the plaza. He heard excited whispers, turned, and saw a half dozen kids approaching down the steps. They flashed knives, pointed at Plesur, licked their lips. He responded by raising the firearm and putting a bullet into the concrete at their feet. They vamoosed back the way they'd come.

"We have to get out of here," said Julia.

"Over there." Plesur pointed to a steel building on the edge of the highest terrace. Three SUVs peeled out of the makeshift garage and vanished into the night.

"Nice wheels," Rook approved.

They hurried up the steps, Julia helping an exhausted David, and came up on the front entrance of the metal building. Rook and Julia leveled their weapons at two thugs eating something unfortunate roasting on a spit. One of them cried out and went for a gun. Julia shot him with the Chancellor and he fell onto the hot coals.

Rook grabbed the other guy, shoved the gun into his mouth, rammed him against the wall, and growled, "Need something fueled and ready to go."

"Take the Hi-Wagon," the terrified man yelped.

"Keys?"

"Number is 323-446."

"Let's go." Rook pushed the guy toward the entrance.

They found the Hi-Wagon, a big-wheeled, Chinese SUV, ready to go. Behind it were a dozen other vehicles.

"Tires, chips, cut 'em and smash 'em," said Rook.

Plesur sank her knife into tires while Julia shot out the

rest. Rook checked the charge level on the Hi-Wagon. Reassured, he waved for the others to pile in.

Then he turned to the garage guard. "Go take care of your buddy."

Swinging into the front seat, Rook tapped the code on the steering wheel and heard the engine hum to life.

They rolled out, bumping up onto concrete, and took off into the dark New Jersey night.

The roughshod road was just a track that occasionally synced with a former street or a piece of highway. They bounced in and out of potholes in between patches of concrete and asphalt.

David sat in the back, eyes closed.

"There was nothing you could have done," Julia said, trying to comfort him.

David shook his head. "No. My fault . . ."

"You did all you could," Rook said. "Right now, we need you to focus. We've got to stay alive. Where do we go?"

David's eyes gleamed with resolve. "Head west for about twenty miles. Across the river there's a local tribe, past the Spillside exit. We can rest there."

The wagon's computers and location systems—useless in uninsured territory—had all been removed.

Rook slipped Ingrid from his pocket and set the sleek little Nokia beside him on the seat. "See if you can wrap your chips around the best route to the Spillside exit."

Ingrid flashed. "My cartographical sensors indicate there is only one viable road to our destination."

"Are we on it?"

"Turn left in .09 miles."

"Thanks, doll."

"You also have a message from Eve Euridiki. She wants to know if you and the pleasure model have survived."

He glanced at Plesur. She nodded.

"Find a secure line, tell her we're alive for the time being. We'll be in touch."

Within a couple of miles, buildings gave way to a dense neotropical forest of low trees and the ubiquitous bamboo that had overrun the increasingly warm northeastern United States.

Plesur sat in the passenger seat, staring listlessly into the dark.

"Are you hurt?" Rook asked anxiously.

Plesur shook her head, flashed him a ghost of a smile. "It's just—I can't remember."

Rook frowned, not understanding.

"When they took the earback away," Plesur said quietly, "nothing made sense. I couldn't do anything. And now this." She brushed the earback Julia had given her. "This is different from the first one. I am someone else now."

"You are Plesur."

"There are many Plesurs," the mod said.

"You're special."

"Because I know things."

"That's not what I meant." He squeezed her hands gently, trying to find the right words. "Those chips might help you, but they're not who you are."

Tears shone in her eyes. "I wanted to help you, Rook. I couldn't . . ."

"From now on, we help each other."

Plesur nodded, swallowing her tears. "Always."

Rook hit the brakes as the track curved to the right, then swung left, and suddenly they came out on open space, miles of marsh with a river running through the middle.

David leaned forward from the backseat. "Just a couple of miles now. Past this golf course."

"Golf course?" Julia looked out at the wild landscape.

"Not for a long time," said Rook.

The water was high, in full flood, carrying debris along as it moved south.

"Where's the bridge?" Rook asked.

"There." David pointed ahead.

Rook followed the ruts along the edge of the river. Vegetation crackled and snapped as the wagon plowed through the narrow road.

Then out of nowhere they drove through a long-abandoned gas station. Trees had taken over, but the long-empty pumps stood silent watch among the vines, sheltered by fragments of walls and some rotted-out vehicles.

On the other side of the old gas station they saw the bridge.

In poor condition, it had gaps and holes along the top of

the span. Many similar incongruous pieces of engineering had been left abandoned in uninsured zones. There was just enough room to get across.

"Not much farther." David tried not to look at the water yawning below them through missing pieces of railing.

"Hold on." Julia applied pressure to the worst of his ragged wounds.

On the far side, a zone of former industrial structures sprawled across the land.

"Turn here," said David. "Then go right."

"I see lights." Julia peered into the murk. "You know these people?"

"I lived with them once, for a couple of months."

"Who are they?"

"Just simple folk trying to survive."

"As long as they can give us shelter for a few hours," Rook said over his shoulder.

He wheeled the SUV through the remains of an industrial plant. Overhead stretched a massive conveyor belt. On either side were ruined buildings.

He hit the brakes, skidding to a stop.

Directly in their path stood a group of people. A big woman in a long skirt and checkered blouse pointed a massive gun at the SUV. Several dozen others had weapons trained on it.

David opened the door and carefully got out. "Mama Red, do you remember me?"

The big woman squinted, then lowered her weapon. "David?"

"Yes."

"Son, you look like you've been dragged through the swamp and back," Mama Red chided.

"These are my friends." David gestured for the others to get out. "We need a place to rest for a few hours. Can you help us?"

"Jesus, what the hell war have you been in?" She peered at Julia, Rook, and Plesur.

"We were held captive by Zato."

The big woman spit a wad of tobacco to the ground. "Had given up all hope on you when you left, figured that might have happened."

"He needs help." Julia braced David as his knees gave out.

"I can see that, missy." The woman looked at his wounds.

She turned to the group of armed men behind her. "They're okay."

The men lowered their rifles and moved quickly to the row of buildings.

"Let's get you cleaned up and fed."

Mama Red led them to a cooking fire surrounded by a dozen or so people of all ages, sitting on a motley assortment of chairs, benches, and concrete blocks. Dressed in mostly patchwork clothes, they made room for the new stragglers.

Within a few minutes introductions were made, the Hi-Wagon had been wheeled into a building to get it out of sight of surveillance drones, and they were sitting by the fire, eating roasted meat.

"This is delicious," Julia complimented, chewing heartily.

"Python," said Mama Red, showing off a fresh hunk waiting to be hung over the fire. "Good eating."

"Caught him when the river got high," said Timi, one of the hunter boys. "Good for a week."

Indeed, the snake was enormous. Two feet thick at the widest point, it had probably been twenty feet long.

This confirmed what Rook knew about the Hudson Valley.

"The snakes came up from Florida about twenty years ago," he told Julia, David, and Plesur. "They're multiplying like crazy."

Julia tried to stifle a grimace. "Tastes like chicken."

"You must eat." Plesur dropped a hunk on Rook's chipped enamel plate and took some for herself.

A girl brought Julia a supply of poultices, which the domme began carefully laying on the worst of David's wounds. The mod picked at his meal, obviously distressed. Julia lay a steaming poultice across a gash in his thigh. "There wasn't anything else you could have done."

"I was all he had." David looked distant.

Julia caught his gaze. "Now you got us."

Rook sat beside Plesur on a wooden bench, soaking in the heat of the fire. His body craved the rich animal protein as it tried to heal the last days' bruises and cuts. He

ate quickly, tossed the bones onto the fire, and asked the Nokia if any service connection was possible.

There was. He set Ingrid the task of contacting Lindi MacEar.

"And stay off the screen."

"Of course," the phone responded. "I have a connection. Taiwan scramble. Open sourcers have broken U.S. security codes. Call is safe."

"Hello?"

"MacEar?"

"Boss, you're still alive!"

"Barely. What do you hear on your end?"

"I've been staying away from the station and my place.

I spoke to Andy Kuehl a couple of hours ago. Says the chief is hiding out in Albany, but the Feds pulled out of the station. There's some big operation going on in New Jersey."

"No shit."

"No real information, but there are military transports in the air down there. Got that from Patrick at air-traffic control in Albany. They're rerouting commercial flights. out of that area. Georgia and Arkansas too."

"Pretty sure we're a high-priority target right now."

"What can I do, boss?"

He was tempted to send the mysterious coordinates to MacEar, see what she could dig up. But it was too dangerous.

"Sit tight and be careful. I'll check in again soon."

Rook killed the call and leaned back against the bench. Filling his stomach had brought on the deep exhaustion that he'd been skirting for days. He had a flash of longing for his own bed, until he remembered it was a pile of ashes in the crater where his house had been. Another casualty of Sangacha's secrets. At least now they had a chance to make it to the coordinates in Plesur's head, maybe find out what the hell this mess was all about.

Through the dancing flames, Rook saw David and Julia sitting close together, talking. The domme seemed to have a soft side under that leather after all. Good, she'd take care of the mod.

Rook felt his eyelids droop. His head dropped to his chest. He was barely aware of Plesur's arms closing around him before a wave of black came sweeping in and he went out like a light.

CHAPTER 11

Rook dreamed of a soft wind blowing across his skin. Of laying on a windswept beach out at Montauk on the Island.

But something tugged at him, and despite everything, his eyes opened. Mama Red was there, and he struggled up on his elbows, thinking they were robbing him in his sleep. Then he saw Plesur standing over him with a big bowl full of steaming liquid.

"He's awake," said Mama Red.

Rook took in the small, neat room, the worn but comfortable cot beneath him. He had no idea how he'd got there.

Mama nodded. "Had the boys carry you in here."

Plesur sat beside him, tired eyes searching his. "You wouldn't wake up."

Mama handed Plesur a stack of clean bandages. "Make sure and use plenty of salve."

"Mama's a doctor." Plesur set the bowl on a wooden side table and started cutting his shirt away.

"No kidding," he murmured.

As she saw his chest, her eyes filled with concern. "You're hurt bad." She pulled the remains of his shirt free.

He looked down and saw a vicious slice below his pectoral muscles, right on the sternum.

He flinched as Mama Red peeled his right pant leg up. "You're lucky you can still walk," she said, shaking her head disapprovingly.

Rook didn't need to look.

Plesur wiped away blood and dirt from his face. "I will take care of him."

"We're still alive, kid." He managed a grin. "But not kicking."

Plesur arched an eyebrow. "Not yet."

Mama Red brought out a jug and yanked out the cork with her teeth.

"Excellent," Rook approved.

"Mama's devil juice," she said with a wicked smile. "Fix ya up real good."

Plesur soaked a rag in it and applied it to the big cut on his chest.

Rook exhaled sharply, the stuff stung like fire.

"Let me see that."

Rook took the bottle and sniffed. Inside was pure ethanol, high-grade white lightning. He took a swig. It tasted like rocket fuel. "Not bad." He drank some more, swished it around in his mouth and spat it out. The middle molar on his right side was loose. His lower lip felt like a sponge thanks to a bamboo strike in the second fight, the flesh around his left eye tender as a raw steak. He was glad mirrors weren't a big feature of Mama Red's décor.

"Homegrown, that's the way it should be." Mama Red applied a big dose to the wounds above his right ankle.

The women cleaned the most serious cuts and abrasions, the worst all being on the lower part of his right leg. By the time the two of them were finished, he was remarkably uncomfortable.

"Feels better, eh?" Mama Red put the cork back in the firewater.

She was right. The burning had been replaced by a cool, anesthetic tingle.

"Good stuff," Rook agreed.

"A family recipe." Mama Red grinned. "Rest now. You'll be safe here for the night."

Rook reached out and clasped the matriarch's ruddy, callused hand. "Thank you."

"Friends of David are friends of mine. Don't give a rat's ass where he come from or how he came into this world. He's as good a man as I ever met." She squeezed Plesur's shoulder on the way out.

Plesur wrapped a wide band of gauze around Rook's chest, her face earnest as she concentrated on her task. Rook had the distinct impression she liked taking care of him. He didn't mind it, either.

He took another swallow of the moonshine, sighing as the heady brew made quick work of his tense and tired muscles.

"I think we have enough bandages," he protested as Plesur ripped open another package of gauze and started wrapping it around him.

"I have to make sure you're okay," she said in a small voice.

He took her hands gently in his.

She was struggling to find words. "When you wouldn't wake up, I didn't know if you were . . . if you would ever . . ."

"I'm right here, Plesur."

She looked at him with such obvious innocence that it melted his heart. "So many are trying to kill us."

"But we're okay now."

"For how long?" She tied off the bandage.

"I don't know."

"We might not have much time together." She leaned forward and kissed him on the lips, gently and then with passion.

Plesur was right. Despite his promises, they might both be dead by morning. Everything had changed since that

first night together, at his house. When? On Tuesday? Had it really been just four days ago?

His entire world had been upended.

He kissed her back.

Their eyes met, and something so pure and sweet sparkled in those blues that it froze the words in his throat.

"You are my man now." She pulled him in close, holding him so gently, he didn't feel any of his bruises. She pulled off her top and let her glorious breasts free.

Yet, some part of him, detached and cool, knew perfectly well that Plesur wasn't natural at all. She'd been crafted in a laboratory by genetic experts, and they had known what they were doing. When his hands found those breasts and held them, their perfection carried through, echoing in deep parts of his brain, where two million years of evolution had honed certain kinds of responses.

"Wait," he whispered. For an instant he hesitated. Was this nothing more than a programmed response, or did she really want him?

One look into her sparkling blue eyes answered his question.

Rook got rid of what remained of his pants.

Plesur was in her element now. This was what she was made for.

Every part of his body hurt so he relaxed and let Plesur take control. She was ready. There was no need for any foreplay.

Watching her in motion, riding him, her hair tousled around her head, Rook thought he had never witnessed anything more beautiful, more real.

It proved impossible for him to keep control for long. But he was hard in an instant after his first orgasm. Plesur settled in for a longer ride and they went on together until she, and then he, came again.

For a few minutes they lay together, her head resting on his chest, but Plesur was not finished.

"My man," she whispered, then moved up and straddled him, bringing her sex down to his mouth. He let the sweet musk fill his senses while he brought her to orgasm.

She slid down to ride again while his hands came around to hold her perfect buttocks, moving with her and around her, the two of them lost in the soft friction of the moment. A red haze filled his vision, he could feel her rising from the plains, climbing the last cliff, and they came together, locked in the moment, and Rook could feel his heart pounding as the ecstasy ebbed and flowed like an endless tide. They fell back, still together, wrapped close, with something pure and crystalline soaring into the night.

With both of them spent, they slept, and for Rook it was deep and dreamless. Circumstance had thrown them together, yet in this cesspool of a world that didn't give a damn, love had found life like a delicate flower struggling through concrete.

Plesur was right, they might not have very long. But if he was going to be killed, at least he'd found something worth dying for.

CHAPTER 12

Rook awoke to find sunlight pouring through a hole in the roof of the shed.

He and Plesur were lying together on a cot in the corner of what had once been some kind of storage building.

Rook looked down at the tousled blond hair resting on his chest and kissed the top of her head.

"We have to get up," he whispered.

She moved a little, then rolled over and stretched her arms.

"G'morning," she said, and sat up. As she ran her fingers through her tangled hair, Rook saw the silvery glint of the earback. He wondered briefly which one it was, and how dangerous it made this gorgeous little female.

She turned and threw herself on top of him.

"I want to wake up every morning with you," she said in between kisses.

Rook was instantly hard as she slid onto him.

"That's a fine how do you do."

Mama Red walked in with a big pot of fresh salve. "If that ain't a cure for what ails you, this might work." She eyed Rook's leg. "You best keep these wounds covered, boy."

"Okay, thanks." Rook adjusted Plesur.

"I mean with these," Mama offered some clean strips of cloth.

Plesur giggled as she rolled clear of Rook.

"We don't have much here, but we got no love for those animals that did this to you." Mama placed a neatly folded stack of clothes on the floor and wiped her hands.

"Thank you, we won't be staying long."

"Anything else I can help y'all with?"

"No. I think we can handle it from here," Rook said.

"Breakfast outside." She turned to go. "I'll leave you to it."

Plesur rolled out of bed and tossed some clothes over Rook's naked body.

Rook sat up, took stock of his bruises and cuts. Felt like he'd been trampled by a herd of buffalo.

With an effort he swung his legs to the floor and held up a faded shirt and jeans. "What do you think?"

"Matches your hair."

The pants were a bit big. But with his belt, he had a place to tuck the gun, and the pockets were good, so he had somewhere to put Ingrid.

The smell of a campfire and roasting food curled into his empty stomach.

"You slept good. Except for the times you didn't." Plesur actually blushed as she slipped on a clean black tank and python pants.

"Not bad for someone who can barely move." Rook pulled her down for a kiss.

"I like moving for both of us."

Plesur helped him out the shack and over to the fire pit, which lay between two larger buildings. The place used to be an industrial park when there was actual industry. Julia and David sat together on a concrete block near the flames, the mod bandaged and looking much improved.

"You, too?" Rook asked David, indicating his bandages.

"Mama works in mysterious ways."

"What's for breakfast?"

Julia held up her plate. "Well, we've got snake, and, oh, more snake."

"My favorite." Rook grabbed a plate and loaded it up. Probably cost half his paycheck to eat this at a swanky restaurant in the city.

Also, some stalks of sugarcane had been cut about a mile downstream, where it had taken root and flourished.

Plesur chewed the end and sucked on the sweet juice. "Tastes like snake."

"How you doing?" David asked Rook.

"One piece, barely. You?"

David grinned. "Hurts like hell."

"Stop complaining." Julia inspected her handiwork on David's arm and side.

Mama Red rounded the corner carrying a well-worn thermos and four cups. "Mornin', got something special for you boys." She set the cups on a table just outside the ring of seats and poured steaming liquid.

"Coffee." Rook breathed happily.

"We ain't uncivilized." Mama handed cups to everyone, though Plesur wrinkled her nose after one sip and slid her cup over to Rook.

He downed them both, polished off the snake, felt the calm of the morning give way to reality.

"We need to hit the road," Rook said grimly.

"Sooner the better," David agreed, glancing at Mama Red. "Only a matter of time before someone comes looking. Mama's hospitality is famous."

"It was a pleasure having David." Mama Red muffled his blond hair.

The mod grinned and blushed.

"What's the plan then?" Julia interjected.

Rook had been thinking about that since waking. "Head north to the New York border. Try to contact Lydia Trenchard, see if she made anything out of the coordinates. Find somewhere we can hide out and stay alive."

"We'll need some supplies for the road." Julia calmly listed materials, as if she'd gone through this drill before. "Water, food, batteries, flashlights, warm clothes."

"No malls around here," said Rook.

"Well, there is one," David said, "but they say it's more like a lagoon."

Rook tensed as shouting echoed in the alleyway past the long metal shed, and two boys came running up.

"Trucks coming," they cried.

Mama Red's eyes flashed. "You know what to do."

The boys ran off and the matriarch gestured to the old factory. "Come with me."

Rook shook his head. "Odds are they're coming for us. We leave, maybe they won't bother you."

Mama Red was silent for a moment, then nodded.

"Let's move!" Rook tossed his plate aside and started leading the others to where they'd hidden their truck.

People dashed in front of them, pouring out of buildings. Rook realized dozens of these folks were here, a whole community carrying belongings wrapped in blankets and hurrying toward a central structure, their stronghold. Like medieval townsfolk under siege, Mama Red's people would defend themselves in their best fortified structure until the danger passed. Clearly this wasn't the first time someone had threatened them.

Rook yanked open the doors of the large shed, ran to their truck, and tried to start it. ERROR—SECURITY OVERRIDE flashed a bright red message on the screen.

"Shit!" Rook slammed his fist on the wheel. "They've changed the keycode."

And if they could change the keycode, they could track the vehicle. "Fuck!" Rook cursed himself for not recognizing that. That he'd been totally exhausted was no excuse. He'd blown their cover and led Zato straight to Mama Red.

"This way!" Julia, pistol in hand, led them out the back and down a concrete roadbed between ruined buildings.

Rook kicked in a door and herded them inside the nearest warehouse. The ground floor was mostly open, with pieces of rock-crushing equipment set in two parallel lines. Above were catwalks in various states of decay, with boxed-off spaces.

Rook was about to try climbing the machines to the

catwalk when the wall exploded, sheetrock and metal flying everywhere. A flatbed truck roared inside, tires screeching like banshees. The machine gun set up on the back let loose with an ear-shattering burst.

"Back door!" screamed Julia.

The four dashed outside and stopped in their tracks.

Two trucks were waiting, a dozen men aboard training so much firepower on them they'd be dead in a second.

The cab door opened and Zato stepped out.

Plesur tensed. Zato wagged his finger at Rook.

"If I were you, I'd tell *la puta* not to go all crazy with her shit." Zato didn't have to point to the machine guns on the trucks.

Rook held Plesur back. They were sickeningly outnumbered.

Julia kept her gun trained on Zato, David by her side.

"You broke up the party, so I bring the party to you." Zato snapped his fingers and two thugs dragged a bleeding, naked man out of the cab and threw him to the ground.

"This piece of shit is my cousin. The fuckup will pay."

Rook could see that Rico had already made some payments. He'd been truly beaten to a pulp.

One of the thugs pulled Rico's head up. Rook shivered, Julia shook her head.

Rico had no nose, no teeth, no lips. His eyes were shut behind massive bruises.

"Watch closely, bitch!" Zato spat eloquently on the concrete in front of Julia. "This is my own flesh and blood. Imagine what I'm going to do to you."

The thugs spreadeagled Rico on the ground. One of them unshipped a two handed rock drill with a two foot long, inchwide bit.

Zato made an impatient little wave of the hand. The guy turned the drill on, it roared and chugged happily. Then he set it between Rico's shoulder blades and drilled slowly through his flesh. Rico's screams were clearly irritating to Zato. He made another gesture and the goon yanked the drill out of Rico's back and set it on his skull.

Julia had had enough. Ignoring the machine guns, she stepped forward and put a bullet into Rico's head. The shrieks cut out and his body stopped writhing.

Zato glared at Julia. "Get in the truck."

David tried to pull her away but two gangsters shoved him back.

"Leave him alone, asshole!" Julia yelled.

"Shut the fuck up." One thug wheeled and slapped her hard.

Rook body-slammed him, groaning as his wounds opened up.

Plesur kicked another in the head, ducking gunfire.

Thundering rotors cut through the chaos. Everyone stepped back as a black chopper swung in and made a fast landing behind the gun-trucks.

The door opened and the trio of Overlord gorillas emerged. They approached slowly, pistols out and slides racked.

"Get the mod," said the nearest.

"So, *ése*," Zato was grinning at Rook. "It's all over for you."

But if Zato thought the party was over, he was wrong. In fact the life of the party was just about to arrive.

A heavy thump struck the roof of the building behind them, sending shock waves into the ground. It was followed by a funny little whine, and Rook felt the hair on his neck stand up. He'd heard that noise before.

He flashed a look to David. *Get ready to run* was the message.

But David was looking up at the roof. Rook followed his gaze and froze.

"Oh, shit."

A massive thing of matte black steel with a row of red eyes crouched above them. It had the shape of a huge tiger, but instead of flesh, it was all steel.

The machine watched the scene below, its catlike head carefully scanning the group. Rows of red sensors finally settled on Plesur.

"What the fuck is that?" Zato and his gang stared up at the thing.

Rook knew that another player had just entered the game, and they'd chosen their favorite pet just for him.

"Get ready," he whispered to Plesur.

Then, in a graceful arc, the hunter robot sprang off the roof straight toward them.

The gang opened up, machines guns hammering away.

Rook grabbed Plesur and started running as bullets ricocheted everywhere. A quick glance over his shoulder showed Julia and David following close behind. Gunfire rose to a crescendo, mingled with screams and the sound of trucks being thrown through walls.

Plesur leaped onto the back of a truck, ripping the machine gun from a shocked gangster and hurling him to the concrete. Rook slid into the driver's seat while Julia helped David into the cab. Plesur had just climbed in the small backseat when Rook spun the truck around and floored it.

Rook looked in the rearview and could scarcely believe his eyes. An SUV was sticking halfway through a steel wall on the far side of the roadbed. Another one had been flipped over on its back.

Bodies lay everywhere, and if he hadn't been terrified he was going to be next; Rook would have enjoyed the sight of Zato being ripped in two by robo-kitty's wide jaws.

He almost turned the truck over as he hit the corner. He cranked the wheel, regained control, and tried not to

focus on the bodies in white suits being thrown eighty feet in the air behind them. The rest of the gang scattered like mice from a tomcat.

But Zato and his gang were not the beast's intended prey. The metallic head swiveled, searching, and locked its sensors.

CHAPTER 13

"Is it still behind us?" Julia craned her neck to look out the rear window.

"Probably." Rook jammed his foot against the accelerator as the truck bumped and bounced over vines, rocks, and debris strewn across the overgrown terrain.

Plesur loaded a cartridge into the machine gun.

David leaned out the window, gun ready, searching for the metal beast. "I can't see a thing."

"Do not slow down!" Julia ordered.

David clung to his seat. "We can't just drive around out here—"

"Fuck!" Rook slammed on the brakes, skidding the

truck across an expanse of cracked asphalt. They came to a stop.

The morning air was still, save for the insect orchestra and unknown sounds of whatever else lived in this hell-hole.

"Holy shit," Julia announced.

Rook had to agree.

Before them stood the remains of a giant mall half buried in the swamp. Through the mist, buildings rose, embedded in the deep water. A Wal-Mart sign lay at an odd angle, crushing the upper story of a Wong's food court. Corroded signs of Shop & Save, Bath & BodyWorks, and Norfolk's tried in vain to lure shoppers who had long since disappeared. Bamboo choked the grand chrome-and-glass entrance, vines curling up enormous escalators frozen in place. Rats scampered through the decay, evading a dark shadow gliding through murky pools of water.

Plesur jumped down and helped Rook as Julia and David got out of the truck, guns drawn and ready.

"They were right, there is a mall here," Rook observed.

What had once been part of a huge parking lot now bordered jungle and swamp that stretched in all directions. The only road he could see was the one they had taken. But going back was not an option.

"You need new bandages," said Plesur, noting stains on his shirt.

"These will have to do," Rook told her.

Julia scowled. "We're in the middle of nowhere."

Rook was checking Ingrid's satellite locator. "We're somewhere northwest of Hackensack."

"I rest my case." The domme stalked away, scanning the desolate horizon.

"Insured territory is about fifteen miles west of here, at the New York border," David said.

"The pleasure model's coordinates are seventy-five miles from there," Ingrid calculated.

"We could be there tonight if the kitty doesn't eat us." Rook wondered what the odds were against that.

"Does anyone know what that thing is?" David asked.

"Robot, obviously," Ingrid spoke up from Rook's hand. "I have a match on Qwiksearch. Cybernetic combat unit reference TYGO440, the ultimate in battlefield decapitation weapons."

Julia paced toward them. "Do you think we lost it?"

"No." Rook was sure of that. The TYGO was definitely military, and Rook had a bad feeling in the pit of his stomach.

Julia shivered. "You think it belongs to those gorillas in the fancy suits?"

"No. Those were top-level executives, Overlords," David told her. "Zato was doing their dirty work. But whoever sent the TYGO didn't want them to get Plesur."

That was true, Rook realized. The Overlords had been working for someone who wanted Plesur alive. So whoever wanted Plesur dead must have sent the TYGO. And only one organization had that kind of pet in its menagerie.

"So who sent it?" Julia scanned the dense jungles.

"Sable Ranch, they control the military," Rook answered.

"They want us dead." Plesur's eyes glinted fire.

Rook turned to face David. "This isn't about you. You can get out of here, go to California. Get a fresh start. Both of you."

Julia glanced at David apprehensively.

David sighed and addressed Plesur. "Whatever you

know, it's powerful. A pleasure mod saving humans, that could change everything."

Plesur smiled gratefully.

"No matter where we go, they'll find us." Angie Bricken, under the Julia overlay, knew the truth of that. "We know too much."

"And we don't know enough," replied Rook. "You've been running for twenty-five years. Only one thing we can do now."

Julia eyed David. "Someone's gotta keep you out of trouble."

David came up with a smile.

Rook nodded. "Let's find a way out of here, call Lydia Trenchard."

"There are service roads that skirt the mall." David pointed to a barely visible stretch of asphalt paralleling what had been a big sports outfitter's store. "We can probably use those to get around the swamp."

"Okay." Rook turned back to the others, but at that exact moment something flashed across the sky to the south, like a football arcing high into the air before descending.

For a couple of seconds he froze, not quite believing what he'd seen. Then he barked, "Back in the truck, come on!" He shoved Julia toward the passenger side, grabbed Plesur by the arm, and swung her up behind Julia.

"Get in! Go, go, go."

Then they all saw it. Something hurtling through the air on a parabolic track, less than a quarter mile distant.

"Shit!" said Julia.

Rook gunned the engine into life.

"It's jumping?" said David. "Those things do that?"

"TYGO440 combines the JMP2 Motion System with a turbocharged 440-horsepower hybrid engine from Matsushita LLC," Ingrid announced helpfully.

"Good to know." David cocked his rifle.

Rook floored it. The truck lurched forward along the cracked, cratered asphalt of the old parking lot and down the service road.

"Can't this thing go faster?" said Julia, looking out the back window.

"No, but it gets great mileage." Rook swerved around the largest of the department stores. Windows flew past, mannequins watching them like ghosts as they sped by.

Suddenly it landed, as lithe as a panther, and was running beside the truck. Rook looked at the speedometer.

They were touching eighty-five miles an hour, but clearly the TYGO440 could go a lot faster if it wanted to.

Rook stared at the incredible killing machine. It was shaped like an eight-foot-long tiger, minus the tail, made of steel, covered in stealthmat, with a belly full of purring engine. Its massive head swiveled and looked right at him with six red eyes set in a row. Rook felt his brain freeze. The thing was terrifying. It sprang sideways and hit the truck with its front feet, rocking the driver's-side wheels into the air, almost turning it over.

The truck slammed down and fishtailed, sideswiping a coffee stand. David and Plesur fired shotguns out the window. The thing took no notice. Rook spun the wheel,

slammed the truck into it, knocking the TYGO through a concrete wall in a cloud of dust and fragments.

"Take that!" yelled David.

But a moment later, the thing exploded out of the wall ahead of them.

"Hold on!" Rook punched the accelerator, but with one leap, the beast landed on top of the cab with a terrifying crunch. The roof buckled as steel claws ripped through metal, peeling it back as if it were opening a can of sardines.

Rook swerved wildly, trying to dislodge it from the truck.

Ahead, a parking garage loomed. WARNING 8 FEET read a battered yellow sign. He whipped the wheel over, tires throwing mud, and they plowed down the entryway and into the dark interior.

The TYGO was left behind, smashed against the concrete wall along with half the truck's roof, torn clean away on impact.

Rook raced the truck through pools of water, past piles of concrete fallen from the ceiling, and long-abandoned vehicles rotting in their parking spaces.

"Over there," screamed Julia, pointing to a semicircle of light leading to an upper level.

The truck shot up the ramp on the far side, plowing past a car that had been left to rust.

They were back out in the center plaza of the mall. Rook floored the pedal, roaring over the remains of dancing fountains, sideswiping an old trolley.

"Got to find a road out of here," he said above the roar of the engine and the howl of the wind through the ripped-open roof.

They turned down an access road between two big box stores, and out of nowhere the TYGO440 dropped right in front of them.

The squeal of brakes, mixed with screams and the beast's engine whine, echoed over the empty mall. With a roar, the truck smacked into the machine head-on, its massive head

exploding through the windshield. Steel jaws snapped at Julia, who dodged back. Plesur unloaded a full clip into its head.

Tires whirled in the mud, they were stuck!

Red eyes burned against black steel as metal jaws snapped inches from their faces.

David pushed Julia to the side and shoved grenades into the thing's open mouth as it gathered itself for another attempt.

Rook whipped the wheel over hard, and the tires found traction, the truck leaping free and flying headlong through a glass wall of the food court. The TYGO fell backward as the grenade exploded, fire gushing from its mouth.

Rook crashed the truck through the tall windows on

the other side of the court. Back on the service road, he turned south. With no windshield, the wind blasted and battered them.

"Did you kill it?" said Plesur, from somewhere in the backseat.

"No idea," said David.

They were parallel now to the ruined Galleria, and Rook was peering ahead, hoping to find the road out of the mall.

Julia and Plesur were staring behind them, looking for any sign of the thing.

"Maybe you did," said Julia hopefully.

"It's dead," said Plesur. "It must be dead."

With a spray of shattered glass, the TYGO leaped out of the Galleria and seized hold of the truck in massive steel jaws.

Rook was jamming the truck into reverse when they felt the vehicle lift off the ground.

Julia pumped rounds from the Chancellor into the monster as the truck went over on its side, the TYGO holding on. They rolled together through a collapsed door and into the Galleria's main lobby. The floor crumbled beneath them, and they fell to the level below.

Rook was waiting for the fuel tank to explode as the truck crashed to a halt.

It was suddenly, eerily quiet.

"You okay?" he said to Plesur. Blood smudged the mod's forehead.

"I think so. You?"

Rook nodded and twisted around to look in the backseat. "Everyone okay?"

"Where's the TYGO?" David helped Julia yank open the cab door.

The whining of servo motors vibrated below the truck.

"It's underneath us!" cried Julia.

They scrambled out, the truck shuddering as the robot moved beneath it.

The hideous head of the TYGO440 punched through the debris and began to haul itself toward them.

"I don't believe this," said Julia.

"Run!" Rook ordered.

They turned and ran down the ruined hallway.

Behind them they heard metal and rubble being pulled apart. Servo motors whined, and Rook thought he heard a different tone. The damned thing had finally sustained some damage.

The hallway curved slowly around to the right.

Along the way he noted a service stairway with a steel door hanging open.

He signaled everyone to stop, then pointed them to the passageway and stairs.

"Got any more of those grenades?" he asked Julia.

The domme handed him the black bag. Inside were guns, grenades, and several pale green metal cylinders.

"Demolition charges." He studied the others, then handed Ingrid to Plesur. "You have to go now. Get as far away as you can. Contact Trenchard and Eve to pick you up."

"What are you talking about?"

"I'll keep it occupied." He handed the bag back to Julia.

"I will stay with you," Plesur insisted.

"No. Whatever happens, you have to stay alive."

Plesur did not like the sound of this.

"Hurry, while it's injured." Rook could feel their window of escape slipping away. "I can lure it here and destroy it."

David gently pulled Plesur toward the stairs. "Okay, man, but you better be right behind us."

"No problemo."

Plesur paused in the doorway. "I will be waiting for you."

"Whatever happens, I will find you." Rook looked deep into her blue eyes. "I . . ."

She kissed him hard, then turned to go.

Rook heard them scramble down the stairs, watched through the rain-streaked windows as Plesur, Julia, and David ran across the muddy road.

He breathed deep and waited. He could hear it, a rasping sound, atop a whistling servo motor that was on its last legs.

He turned and saw the TYGO limping toward him, having lost its right front paw. Something was also wrong with its back, but it was still more than capable of running him down.

"Here, kitty, kitty. That's right. Got a nice surprise for you."

He twisted the top of three explosives.

The TYGO440 lurched up to him, the massive head swinging from side to side. He observed that two of the eyes had been knocked out, but the others still gleamed with cybertronic activity.

"You want a piece of me?" He aimed his gun at one of the eyes, daring the machine to take him down, ready to jam three explosive charges down its throat.

But he had it wrong. With a wheeze from the broken

servo motor, the robot slowly settled itself on its steel haunches, keeping Rook backed against the wall.

Rook moved left but it blocked him. He feinted right, but the metal creature easily batted him back, red eyes fixed on him. It was blocking his escape, playing with him like a mouse.

"What the fuck?" He heard a loud click and looked in his hand. "Oh, shit."

He tossed the charges as far as he could and hit the floor.

White light flashed through his brain as the building went up in a fireball.

CHAPTER 14

They were hurled forward as if by a giant hand as the mall collapsed behind them and a fireball mounted into the sky with a small mushroom cloud.

"Rook!" Plesur pulled herself from the wet ground and was running toward the smoking rubble.

David jumped to his feet and held her back. "Plesur, the entire building has collapsed!"

"Let me go!"

"No one could have survived that," said Julia quietly, picking up the Chancellor.

The smoke and dust were clearing now. They could see a massive crater where the food court had been. Tons of

debris had fallen from the roof and the second story of the Galleria.

Julia gently put a hand on Plesur's shoulder. "There is nothing we can do. We have to keep going."

Grief-stricken, Plesur didn't move. "He can't be dead."

The sorrow in the p-mod's voice was so obvious, Julia suffered a spasm of sympathy. "He was a good man."

"He saved all of us," David said. "He gave us—you—a chance. We can't waste it."

Julia glanced at David. "That fireball had to be visible for twenty miles. Who knows who else has seen it."

Plesur took one last look at the ruined mall, then faced her friends. "Which way?"

"Check the satellite map," David suggested.

Plesur slipped the Nokia from her pocket, looked at it uncertainly, and handed it to Julia. It lay there cold in the domme's hand.

"What's wrong with this thing?" Julia kept punching at the black screen.

David peered over her shoulder. "Maybe the power's dead."

They moved on and emerged from the alley to a rear parking lot, on which weed trees and bamboo were starting to get a grip. Halfway along lay a human skeleton, minus the arms, chewed off by animals. The bones were half in, half out of a faded anorak. Eroded rubber boots projected from drifted plastic and dirt.

"We head north," said Plesur. "Toward the border. Maybe Lydia Trenchard will help us."

"Then what?" Julia scowled. "Walk into some kind of trap?"

"You got a better idea?"

The domme hesitated. Her instincts were screaming at her to just shut up, to let the mods fend for themselves and get the hell out of here. But that was Mistress Julia's voice, the dominatrix persona designed with the lack of empathy required to whip clients until they bled. Angie Bricken, on the other hand, wanted to help Plesur, and not just because it might help her find out what had happened to Mark. She had spent the last twenty-five years alone, running, not trusting anyone. In the last two days, she had saved and been saved by people who barely knew her, pleasure models who weren't even supposed to be human. She wasn't sure what the hell it was, why she was attracted to David. Maybe it was his quiet courage. But

she hadn't had these feelings since Mark. For the first
time since he died, she had a goal. She knew it was impossible for her to leave David and Plesur now. "Look,
I have to tell you something. I know where those coordinates are."

"What?" David studied her curiously.

"I have a house a few miles from there."

"Why didn't you say something before?" asked Plesur.

"I was freaked out. I didn't know if I could trust you."
Julia glanced at David shyly.

David considered the new information. "How do we
get there?"

"I know someone who can help us."

They hurried into the dwarf forest of giant weeds and
bamboo.

"Damn phone!" Julia shook the Nokia, trying to get a
signal.

They'd gone about half a mile when a rumbling sound
broke across the land, which quickly resolved into the thud
of rotors as a big helicopter swooped up from the south.

"Shit, get undercover!" Julia grabbed the mods and pulled them beneath a canopy of bamboo.

The chopper circled over the mall, then landed.

"They're checking for survivors," said David.

"Rook," Plesur murmured in a voice drained of life.

"There's lettering on that chopper." Julia squinted.

"FBI," said David, blessed with the fabulous vision of a p-mod.

"Christ, let's keep going."

After about twenty minutes they came out of the forest onto the shore of a lake. On the other side were more trees, but beyond them, in the distance, they could see buildings.

"Have to get around the water," said David.

"Let's go west." With Rook gone, Julia had assumed the role of leader.

The sun gleamed against the silent tears streaming down Plesur's cheeks as they pressed on along a trail that wove in and out of bamboo and patches of dry land.

"C'mon, phone, wake up!" Julia tried yet again to get Rook's Nokia to cooperate.

"Ingrid," said Plesur.

"What?"

"Her name is Ingrid."

Julia held up the phone. "Ingrid, can you hear me?"

The Nokia emitted a small, tentative light.

"Rook gave you to us now," Julia explained. "You have to help us."

"If he has given me away, I calculate a 96.8976 percent chance he is dead."

"The TYGO," Plesur told Ingrid.

"I will allow call connections, temporarily," Ingrid's smooth voice consented.

"Thanks." Julia quickly dialed her answering service.

"You have nine unanswered calls."

"Hold them. No, list them."

They were all clients of Mistress Julia's. She deleted them, then asked Ingrid to dial Dr. Jimmy's number. He was the doctor, he could fix anything.

A few moments later he picked up. "Jools? Where the 'ell are you?"

"Uninsured New Jersey, pretty crazy down here."

"Heard they got alligators and cannibals, going right back to the Stone Age."

"I can vouch for the alligators. Look, Jim, I need some help. I'm with two friends and we have information that might be of real interest to you."

"You got my attention."

"We need to get someplace where we can get cleaned up and hide out."

"'Ide? From what?"

"I can't say much more over open lines. But I'm pretty sure that snake in the bottle you were talking about?"

"Yeah."

"Someone let it out."

Dust, fragments, pieces of steel rained down, and with it came the stench of burnt metal and concrete.

Rook lay there, not moving. Good news was that he wasn't dead—yet. Bad news was he had one ton of robot on top of him.

The machine rattled and shook. Front legs tensed and rose. Its head was charred and pocked full of dents. Only

a few of the sensors had survived. But they were damaged enough to allow Rook to shimmy away from beneath the thing.

He scrambled through the debris and surveyed the remains of the mall. It hadn't been much to look at before, but at least it had walls and a roof. Rook had completely demolished it.

"Jesus, you think I used enough explosives?"

By all accounts, Rook himself should be scattered across the wreckage in a few dozen pieces. The TYGO had saved his life!

With a faint grinding, the head turned to watch him. He took three steps back. The machine lifted itself to its feet, with a raspy whine from the servo motors.

He stopped. It stopped. He stood there, and a moment later it sank back onto its haunches, then down onto its belly, if a machine could be said to have such a thing.

"Some day, eh?" The red optics studied him, but otherwise there was no response.

After a few minutes, Rook sat down with his back against the rubble. The other shoe was bound to drop soon.

He hoped Plesur was safe, hoped Julia and David could help her reach those coordinates. He missed Plesur already and found he didn't want to think about what had happened the night before. It was all too unbearably sweet, and now, over.

Could pleasure models fall in love? Did they have the capacity for that much emotion? Even if Plesur loved him, she was an illegal life-form, engineered to be dead in ten years anyway, if something else didn't kill her first.

The questions roiled in his mind but one thing was certain: the light he'd seen behind those blue eyes. That light had been genuine, and he knew that for him that meant more than anything.

But would he ever see it again?

A distant rumble broke in on these ruminations. The rumble soon grew into a steady throb, then into the unmistakable sound of a chopper arriving.

Through the broken roof of the Galleria, he saw it swing

in and hover, the big white letters FBI on the side, then descend, landing in a dust storm of stone and ash.

The quiescent TYGO440 raised up and sat on its haunches, for all the world like a tiger.

Five minutes later three agents marched down the only set of intact stairs. They seemed unsurprised to see him.

"Well, look what the cat dragged in." One of the agents surveyed the scene.

The one in command raised a small hand unit and directed a laser light at the TYGO's optical system. In response, it sat down and the red lights faded. "Jesus, Venner, I've seen corpses buried for two weeks look better than you."

"Nice to see you, too, Agent Skelsa. Here to do a little shopping?"

"What a fucking mess." Skelsa's bionic eyes observed the ruins and the TYGO.

"We've been playing."

"You've been invited to a party, SIO Venner." The other agents hoisted him up the stairs and into the chopper.

"Nice. Where are we going?"

"You'll find out when you get there."

CHAPTER 15

"You get to this rest area, Jools, and wait there. The truck will find you." That's what Jim had told her.

They'd met Jim's truck at a Charge Center near Spillside, after climbing back into the insured world over a concrete wall. They'd slept in the truck while it ran up highway 287 and dropped them on the edge of the Catskills.

"There's nothing here." David waved his hand at the thick forest on either side of the road.

"These are the precise coordinates," Ingrid insisted when Julia checked with the Nokia.

"Least it's not a swamp." Julia tried to ease the back

pains and leg cramps, the cost of the kind of living they'd endured the last three days.

The light was fading, it would soon be dark, and they were obviously a long way from anywhere.

"Hope this guy is as good of a friend as you think," David said.

Plesur checked his bandages. He was already beginning to heal. "Your wounds are mending well."

"Patented p-mod immune system." David grinned.

Plesur managed a small smile and tied the bandage on his left arm. "Good while it lasts."

David studied her sad face. "Life is sweet, Plesur. We have to go on, live it while we can."

"I don't know if I can anymore."

"You can, believe me. Time goes by very fast."

"And slow."

"Yes. And slow." He smiled. "You have friends now."

Julia watched the mods, surprised by the flutter of jealousy in her chest. Of course there would be a connection. And caring for David probably gave Plesur some comfort, now that Rook was gone. Julia retrieved the black bag full of weaponry. Having seen those slim green, cylindrical demolition charges in action, she decided to take a closer look at what she had. Perched on a pair of rocks sticking up out of the weeds and brush, she explored the bag. Meanwhile mosquitoes gathered and began exploring her. She swatted

them away and counted seven grenades, three with orange rings around the top that indicated something or other. She had two pistols, one a Glock 7 and the other an unknown make, with no marks, and also a 7.62 mm. She had four clips for the Chancellor, plus spare clips for the Glock and a box of one hundred rounds of 7.62 ammo, unopened.

"Santa bring you everything you wanted?" asked David, sitting down beside her.

"I've been very naughty this year."

"Really? I hadn't noticed."

"How's she doing?" Julia glanced at Plesur, sitting a few yards away, arms wrapped around her knees.

"Difficult for her." David sighed. "Took me a few years to deal with my man dying."

"Taken me my entire life," Julia said.

"Plesur is tough."

"But can she survive all this?" Julia felt as if she were asking that question for all three of them.

"I did, and worse." He gazed into her eyes. "Thanks to you."

She squeezed his hand, warm and comforting. "Happy to be of service."

David was easy to like. Something about him was genuine. Plesur as well, actually. Julia had plenty of experience with pleasure mods but had never really considered that they could have real emotions, feelings.

When she'd asked him if he'd ever had sex with women, he'd smiled and said yes. At the fight clubs, women paid to fuck the winners, and they liked them sweaty and even bloody.

"So," she said, putting the clips into a row on the rock, "you belonged to a man. You prefer men?"

Without a moment's hesitation David said, "I prefer you."

That was David, direct and simple. Maybe all Davids were like that.

Mistress Julia took that in stride, but Angie was a little freaked by it.

David saw a frown on the classically beautiful features. "What's wrong?"

"That stupid kid."

"Rico?"

"He was such an easy play."

"You did the right thing."

Angie wasn't convinced, but she was exhausted by everything that'd happened. More than that she was horrified by the savage glee she'd felt when Julia finished wrapping up Rico the way a spider does a fly.

"You are not really typical of, you know, your kind?" Come on, Angie, she thought, that was pretty close to inarticulate.

But David understood. "I've met a lot of us, the Davids. We're not very complicated. The upgrade made a big difference. Made me more, I don't know the word . . ."

"Sophisticated?"

"Okay."

"Learning is very different for us," David told Julia. "Before I was upgraded, I didn't think about anything. I just performed. Then it all got more complicated."

"Complicated, that's just life."

"That's all we want," said David.

She had to look away from those clear blue eyes. Less than a decade of living, and David knew exactly who he was. Fifty years, and she had Julia and Angie fighting it out in her head, wrestling for control. Neither of them was a whole person.

Plesur had got up, paced over to sit beside them.

"It was easier before," she said. "Without so many feelings."

"But it's better to be able to feel them, don't you think?" David asked gently.

"Yes."

There was silence after that, and Julia put the weapons and ammo back in the bag.

Before she'd finished they heard engines, somewhere out in the woods. The sound got louder quickly and there were lights, then suddenly a pair of balloon-tire ATVs rolled out of the trees and stopped beside them.

"Julia?" said the driver of the nearest vehicle. She wore a helmet that covered her features, but something about her was familiar. Julia assumed she'd probably seen the woman at Jim's compound.

"Right." Julia gathered her bag and stood. "Friends of Dr. Jimmy."

"Come on then, we'll take you back to the Fort."

The driver patted the spacious seat. "I'm Hedda. You and the Pammy come with me. Silvie will take the David."

The ATVs were fast and powerful, and they used a network of narrow trails, one vehicle wide, that wound through a valley choked with dark hemlocks. They drove through the ruins of former communities where abandoned houses were arranged along now vanished roads and streets. These melancholy clusters of ruin brought home to Julia how profound the Emergency had been. This whole area, hundreds of square miles in a densely populated part of the country, had been proscribed and emptied of people.

Just when Julia's ass was getting tired of bouncing around on the seat, Hedda stopped at a gate manned by heavily armed guards. A fifteen-foot fence with security cams stretched in both directions.

Julia caught looks from David and Plesur. They were all thinking the same thing: who the hell were these people?

Inside the compound, a road ran beside cultivated fields that sprawled as far as the eye could see. Acres of crops spread out, dark leaves shining in the setting sun. Julia gritted her teeth as the ATVs negotiated the rough dirt track.

An odd detail caught her eye. In a humped-up bank of ground off to the right, she observed rectangular, horizontal slits, jet-black against the dark gray background. Like a military bunker, she thought.

The ATV came around a corner, and up ahead was a massive piece of bare rock, at least the size of a house.

The track went around it and curved past a second and a third, until it ended at several structures.

A pair of dogs barked and ran out to greet them. A door opened, a man came outside.

"You got 'em, Hedda?" he said.

" 'Course" was the response. The ATVs slid to a halt, idled, and cut out. Julia and the others got off and turned to meet their host.

"Welcome to the Calann Ranch. I'm Rory Calann." He shook Julia's hand firmly.

"Hi, I'm Julia. This is David, and Plesur."

"Welcome."

Julia glanced at her companions and saw they were just as surprised by their host as she was.

Rory Calann was tall, slim, hard-muscled, sporting an array of military tattoos. He had level green eyes and a thin mouth set in a pretty-boy face. His black hair was

pulled back in a ponytail, revealing high cheekbones. A good-looking young man in his twenties.

Hedda and Silvie removed their helmets, silky black hair flowing free. They were both Lotuses, bestselling Chinese mods.

"Guess Jim didn't tell you about us." Hedda grinned as a handful of other people came out of the house to greet them.

Plesur, David, and Julia stared in shock.

They were all pleasure models.

CHAPTER 15

It was amazing how short a distance lay between the uninsured world of swamps and gang lords, and the glittering towers of Manhattan. They'd been in the air for about fifteen minutes, and now the sleek FBI chopper was coming in to land on a massive deck on top of an office tower.

The visual effect was vertiginous, Rook found he was holding on to his seat as the chopper dropped through the forest of huge towers. The sparkling city spread beneath him like some exquisite toy as they spiraled onto the landing deck.

No sooner were the wheels down and locked when Agent Skelsa jumped out, signaling Rook to follow.

The lights were so bright it was hard to tell if it was day or night. They walked across the deck toward a set of sliding glass doors.

The air-conditioning inside hit Rook like a blast of arctic air. Hundreds of people milled about a grand ballroom in a blur of expensive suits and glittering jewelry, sipping champagne from gleaming crystal flutes. Pink and white balloons floated from the floor all the way up to the domed glass ceiling, setting off profusions of red and pink roses dripping from centerpieces, pedestals, and buffet tables. A band played in the corner, a smartly

dressed conductor jiving and shaking to the big-band beat. A colorful HAPPY 100TH BIRTHDAY sign hung below the bandstand.

Rook almost burst out laughing. This was surreal.

He was marched through the manicured crowd, looking worse than something stuck on the bottom of their designer shoes.

"Champagne?"

A slight, blond-haired man, maybe thirty, trim and well-groomed, offered Rook a brimming flute.

Rook took the drink and downed it, then noticed that Skelsa and his goons had disappeared.

"An honor to finally meet you, Detective Venner."

"Wish I could say the same." Rook studied the young man, elegantly decked out in black tux and tails. Definitely some cosmetics here, chin, eyes, probably the nose, too.

"Forgive me. I am Fredrick Beckman."

Rook, beyond surprise after the last few days, sighed and grabbed another flute from a passing tray of drinks.

"You are an honored guest here," Beckman said.

"All this for me, you shouldn't have."

Rook stood out like a bug on a white rug. He was filthy, his clothes ripped to shreds, bruises and welts covered his body, dirty bandages streaked with dried blood. Yet no one gave him any kind of a dirty look. No one seemed to care. They were all having a grand time, chatting, drinking, and dancing in this sky palace.

"I, for one, am glad to see you in one piece." Freddie raised his glass in a toast, shrugged, and took a sip when Rook didn't reciprocate.

"And who should I thank, you?"

"For starters. There are things you need to know, important things."

"Let's start with where I can get a real drink."

Beckman chuckled. "Everything is going to be just fine."

"That's a relief," Rook said sarcastically. "You going to tell me what all this is about? Sangacha was going to betray you, give information to Trenchard and Perez. That it?"

"Oh, you mean the coordinates. We know all about that."

"You try to kill me and then bring me to a party. What do you want?"

Freddie laughed. "I'd like to introduce you to someone. She's dying to meet you. Come."

He led Rook through the partying dignitaries. He felt like a beggar at the Feast of Fools.

The crowds parted like the Red Sea to reveal a slim woman, perhaps five foot five, talking with several men. She was wearing a simple but elegant black dress and had her straight white hair in an equally simple shoulder-length style. Only her massive emerald on a platinum ring reflected the power radiating from her small figure. Her eyes caught Rook's and her face lit up in a dazzling smile. Excusing herself from her guests, she strode to him like a queen in complete control of her kingdom. She looked not a day older than forty, but he was certain that she had many more years than that.

"Hello, Detective. I am Louisa Marion." The icy voice belied the perfect smile. He felt as if he were being scanned by Skelsa's robot.

There were a great many things he wanted to say, but none of them came to mind.

"Happy birthday."

"Why thank you."

He felt as if she wanted to put him on the buffet table, pick him apart, see what was inside. "I'm so glad you could attend my party."

"Sorry, my suit is in the cleaners."

"I'm sure a nice hot shower and clean clothes will do wonders. You'll be good as new. Better." The Texas accent gave her words a certain warmth, even though Rook knew she didn't give a damn for his personal comfort and well-being.

"Why did you blow up my house? Why'd you try to kill me?"

She laughed, a brittle sound. "No, no, Detective, we don't want to kill you."

"I told you the situation was complicated, Venner," Beckman interjected. "But things are getting back under control."

Rook played dumb. "What things?"

"You're not stupid, Rook." Louisa pinned him in her gaze, then her face shifted to a smile. "You don't mind if I use your first name, do you?"

"Knock yourself out."

"You knew Sangacha was going to be a difficult assignment, and you did your best with it. But there are loose ends that need to be tidied up."

"It's all about her, isn't it?"

"Do you know where she's gone?" asked Louisa Marion.

"No. I told them to run, get as far away as possible. California would be my bet."

"That would be unfortunate." Her voice sounded like ice falling into cold water.

Rook had the feeling that "unfortunate" meant Louisa Marion was prepared to unleash a whole stable of robokitties to get what she wanted.

They were interrupted by a phone warble.

"Excuse me." She turned halfway around, offering her profile to Rook while she took the call.

"Judd, thanks for calling. . . . Yes, it has been, but that will be over pretty soon. . . . Well, thank you. I know, one hundred used to seem like a very big number. Not anymore. . . . Yes. And you, too. Look, on the Mexican trade bill? I want to meet with you and some of the Democrats. We have to get a bipartisan bill, and I have the feeling I'll be able to convince enough of them to see things our way."

She turned back to Rook. The icy blue eyes studied him for a moment. "Tell me, Detective, what do you think I should do?"

"Beats me, I've never been to Mexico."

"I mean about the pleasure model."

"She has no idea why those coordinates are so important, or what Taste Imperative means," Rook said. "Neither of us do. What if we forget all about it, go live under a rock somewhere far out of your way?"

"That's all very romantic, but impossible."

"All I want is to stay alive and keep her safe," Rook said smoothly. "I'm sure you have ways of keeping an eye on us, making sure we don't meet up with anyone who can tell us what those two words mean."

"No one would ever tell you that. And whoever did, well, you know how messy that is." Louisa Marion moved toward the double high windows overlooking the cityscape of Manhattan. "This is not the life I would have chosen for myself. But circumstances demanded that I step up and make sure our country survived. We went through a very rough time."

"The Emergency."

She turned back to look at him, and he felt something sinister rising from the fanatical gleam in those blue eyes.

"America was built on cheap energy, and when energy

was no longer cheap, well, we started going downhill. My husband saw that, and he knew what we had to do. Unfortunately, there were people that didn't care about the nation, people who only cared about making their own fortunes. They killed him."

She paused, stepped closer to Rook, and looked right into his eyes.

"And I killed them. I had no choice."

"And you used men like Sangacha."

She smiled for a moment, but not maliciously.

Rook swallowed. He had seen killers of all kinds, from the cold to the crazy. But this woman was in an another league entirely.

"They would have destroyed this country," she said. "I couldn't let that happen."

"What do you want from me?"

"I would like you to continue your career, Detective."

Rook was stunned. Could he dare trust these words? "And what, work for you?"

"You already work for me, whether you know it or not. Now, I want you to take a hot shower and rest. We will meet again, and then you will tell me everything."

"Everything?"

"Oh, yes." She smiled. "Everything."

She strode away, happily chatting with several dignitaries. One of the tuxedos grabbed Rook by the arm, manhandling him down a passageway. He shoved Rook into a large apartment boasting a massive antique desk, a gorgeous red Oriental rug, and sweeping views out of the wall-length window. Much better than his last cage, Rook thought.

The guy in the tux dumped a pile of towels and fresh clothes on the bed. He leaned down to glare into Rook's face. "You smell like shit."

"No doubt about that. You got a minibar in here?"

The door closed behind tuxedo man. Rook sat and tried to get a grip on his emotions. He didn't know how long he had to live, and he was well aware that these people played for keeps. They had spent a small fortune deploying that machine to hunt him down, and Rook couldn't figure how they were going to get their money's worth.

He was just an SIO on a case that he really wished he'd never shown up for. Then he thought of Plesur and his heart ached from the one precious night they had spent together. Those blue eyes, full of passion, smiling at him in the morning light, trusting him completely. The way she kissed him as if it were their last moment on earth. It had all got to him, as no woman ever had before.

A woman under permanent official sentence of death. A woman who could only qualify as property, not as a citizen.

He remembered Plesur grabbing the front of his shirt in the cab as they headed for the clinic, the desperation and hope in her voice.

Plesur still get smart.

It wasn't just the earback that made her special.

How could anyone say that she wasn't a person? Or deny her the chance to lead some kind of reasonable life?

But just when he'd seen the truth about Plesur, everything else had taken a sharp turn into fog and shadow. He might not come out of here alive, might never solve the mystery of those coordinates, of Taste Imperative, might never get a chance to wake up with Plesur beside him again. The promises of going back to his career didn't ring true. The only certainty was that whatever Marion was planning for him, he could never go back to the way things were.

CHAPTER 17

"How many of you live here?" Plesur asked as she took in the array of pleasure models. Aside from Hedda and Silvie, there were AfriQueens, Blossoms, a Pammy, a couple of Michaels, and some others that she had never seen.

"Mods?" asked Hedda. "I think we're about fifteen now."

"I'm Kaleesa," said an AfriQueen.

"Hi." Julia shook her hand. "Julia."

"Nice to meet you." David extended his hand to Rory, hesitating for a moment when he saw the scar running up the left side of his throat.

"Been fighting a long time. Got real good at it," Rory said. "Looks like you know what I'm talking about."

"Zato."

"Scum doesn't even deserve to be considered human." Rory's eyes glazed with hate. "Should be dog meat."

"Cat food would be about right," Julia said.

Rory held David's gaze for a moment, then spoke to Julia. "Jim'll be over later. He said to take good care of you. You're a special friend."

Rory had a nice smile, was missing a tooth, bottom front. She noticed a second scar, a small one, that ran along his right cheek atop the bone.

An old truck, painted in camo, rolled into the yard. Two young men jumped down and pulled a rocket launcher off the back and carried it into the barn on the far side of the yard.

"You've got weapons," said Julia.

Rory smiled. "Only way the Calann family has stayed alive out here. Government's tried to destroy us a couple of times now. Last time we gave as good as we got."

The two black and white border collies at Rory's side started barking.

"Well, Nip and Tuck are ready to eat, I expect you guys are hungry, too. Come on in, Mavis has some supper cooking."

"Thanks for helping us," Julia said.

"It's what we do," Silvie said. "See you at dinner."

She and Hedda zoomed off on the ATVs, heading toward the fields of crops.

"Quite a farm," David said.

Rory looked at his crop proudly. "Turnips. Seventy-five acres' worth."

"You make a good living with those?" asked Julia.

"The turnips are an acquired taste, but the leaves have the highest THC content I've ever found."

Julia blinked.

"Come on inside." Rory headed back toward the main house.

Now that Julia, Plesur, and David had officially been greeted, the collies moved in to sniff them out. They were fragments of constant motion, bright eyes, black noses, bushy tails wagging.

The other mods said their hellos and went about their business, back to the other buildings and into the fields.

Julia had absorbed some details of the building now. The sprawling farmhouse had been built of wood over many eras of construction. But the core was built with defense in mind, dug into the ground and made of stone with slits for windows. Two huge rocks, fifty feet high and a hundred across, stood at either end of the house, like bookends holding up a collection of vintage hardbacks of all different sizes.

"I can see why they called this the Fort," Julia said.

Rory Calann laughed. "It's a good defensible position, that's for sure. We protect our own, even have a full medical facility on-site. My brother is a surgeon."

"This place is amazing," Plesur said. "I didn't know mods could live like this."

Rory grinned. "We stay off the radar."

Inside, it was a country house, with rambling halls and rooms of all shapes and sizes that seemed centered on a big kitchen, where a pair of mods were at work.

"Hi, I'm Mavis," said a brunette, a former Brandy model.

"Chicken potpies tonight!" A Frederico covered in flour rolled out biscuit dough on the counter. "With extra pot. Hope you're hungry."

"I guess we will be," said Julia.

Plesur and David trailed behind her, silent, soaking it

all in. This was a little surreal for Julia, she could only imagine what her mod friends were feeling.

"Bet you'd like to clean up before dinner," Rory offered.

"Dying for a shower." Julia felt her tired body relax at the thought of hot, steaming water.

Hidden down a labyrinth of twisting hallways, Rory showed them a suite of rooms with polished wood floors and white walls. The house had clearly expanded as more space was needed, rooms added wherever they fit best.

Plesur and David gratefully went into their rooms, and Julia did the same. She ripped off her leather the second she was alone and jumped into the best shower of her life, relishing getting clean after the days spent in rainstorms, alligator pits, car wrecks, and swamps.

When she came out, drying her hair with a fluffy white towel, her leather had been removed, and in its place was a clean set of jeans and a cotton shirt, plus a pair of moccasins. Everything fit perfectly, and she went out to thank whoever had done this.

Instead she found dinner was being served in a large dining room with a table surrounded by almost thirty men and women.

"Jim!" Julia ran to her friend, giving the eccentric criminal a hug.

"Nice to see you, too, Jools." Jim grinned. "Lookin' good."

Julia slid into the open seat between Jim and David, running her hand through her damp hair and sighing happily. "I feel like a whole new person."

David studied her transformation. "Country girl suits you."

She smiled, ridiculously pleased by the compliment. "Not so bad yourself."

In jeans, a denim shirt, and brown leather boots, he looked ready to settle into life at the Fort. Clean bandages peeked out of his collar and cuffs.

"Help yourself." Mavis waved at the trays of food in the middle of the table.

"It's delicious." Plesur, sitting next to David, leaned over and passed Julia the salad bowl. A shower and a change of clothes had done her good, but her eyes were red and she looked exhausted.

"Thank you for your hospitality," Julia said to Rory, who was sitting across from her.

"Friends of Jim's are friends of ours." He poured some

wine for Julia and refilled Jim's glass. "Done a lot of business together over the years."

"Cheers." Jim clinked his glass against hers. "Jools, David told me a bit, said you lost someone this morning."

"Rook Venner, SIO on the homicide squad in Kingston." Julia glanced at Plesur. "Died to protect us. He was a good man."

"Honest cop. Fuckin' rarity up there in Kingston, I'll tell you that." Jim snorted. "So you took my advice and met our ex-president, eh, Jools?"

"I picked Plesur up from the Frog, took her to see him."

"Heard that didn't end too well."

"Venner showed up, said two words, and Marion, he went berserk, started screaming, and . . ." Julia stopped, afraid she might puke at the memory.

"And what?" Jim prompted.

"His head exploded."

"What, shot by a sniper?"

"Explosive chip. Venner, he found this scrap of paper at General Sangacha's."

"Your other dead client." Jim raised a bushy eyebrow.

Julia nodded. "And Plesur's owner."

"Fuck." Jim whistled.

"So Venner reads two words off this paper, Taste Imperative, and ten seconds later I'm wearing Marion's brains."

"Taste Imperative," Jim repeated. "Sounds government. Always give things nice little names that nobody else can figure out."

Julia told him the rest, Lydia Trenchard, the Latins, Mama Red, the TYGO. When she'd finished, she had the attention of everyone at the table. Quite the dinner conversation.

"And you jumped off the friggin' roof. Amazin'!" Jim shook his head. "Zato was a real bastard."

"You've had dealings with him?" said Rory.

"Now and then, but cash in advance. And I never go in person. He had a nasty habit of feedin' people to his crocodiles."

"Alligators," Rory corrected.

"All right, what's the bleedin' difference?"

"Gators have a wider jaw, slightly different arrangement of teeth."

"Christ, Rory, the stuff you got in your 'ead."

For a moment Julia's gaze rested on Plesur, who felt her attention and looked up. So much had happened to her, it was amazing she was holding up so well. The Pammy's eyes moved to Rory and Mavis, who sat beside each other, golden bands glinting on their ring fingers.

"You're married?" asked Plesur.

"Nearly three years." Mavis beamed.

A human and a mod, actually married. Julia stared in amazement.

"I was planning to pass through here on my way to Canada, but then I met Rory." Mavis squeezed his hand. "Been helping run the Fort ever since."

David looked at the table full of free pleasure models. "How did you all end up living here?"

Jim nodded at Rory. "He's been running an underground railroad for mods, the Fort's famous for 'elping folk like you find a better life. Before Rory, it was his dad who ran this place."

"Took over for him ten years ago," Rory said. "Some

mods like it here so much, they end up staying. We're all free citizens here."

"You all have upgrades," Plesur noted.

"That's the way it works," Hedda, sitting at the other end of the table, spoke up. "Without the upgrade, you can't escape. Hell, the word's probably not even in our vocabulary."

"Why Canada?" asked Julia.

"Upgraded mods are given modified citizenship," Mavis said. "They can get jobs, health care, live in the open. Not everyone up there approves of it, but for a mod it's better than being a slave."

"It must be dangerous to get through the wall into Canada," said David. "They've got hunter robots, right?"

Julia shivered. She'd had enough robots to last her a life-time. The image of the TYGO tossing half a man through the air, spilling blood and viscera in a stream, flashed in her mind. Hopefully Rook hadn't suffered something like that before the explosion.

"We've been running the Freedom Road for quite a while now," Rory was saying. "We know who to pay off."

Plesur glanced from Rory to Jim.

"I have coordinates, put in my head by the man who owned me. I don't know what's there, but I have to go."

"Whatever she knows, it's important," David added. "Sable Ranch has been chasing her for days."

Excited by this bit of information, Jim leaned forward. "And just where are the coordinates?"

"On the ridge," Julia told him. "Just north of us."

Jim went pale. "Behind the wire?"

"Yes."

"Four miles north, past the High Point, there's this old facility. Chain-link fence, razor wire, has these signs, black skull and crossbones. Fuckin' serious lookin' stuff." Jim was torn between excitement and apprehension. "Four months ago, they came in and started fixing the place up. Set off the ol' red alert for us, as you might imagine."

Angie thought of Dip and all the others in Jim's tribe of lost children. She imagined them running around putting equipment on, getting out guns, loading ammo clips, scanning the skies for intruders.

"That's why you were out in the trees that night," Julia realized.

She remembered the explosion, the mean-looking gunship.

"You want another sign, darlin'?"

"What do you mean?"

"Your friend, Detective Venner. The explosion we saw that night. That was his place getting toasted."

Julia sat back, trying to process all this information. Four months ago. There had been a change in Sangacha about that time. He seemed edgy, ordering stronger punishment. Whatever Sable Ranch was doing up there, it scared him enough to dredge up a conscience.

Jim poured some more wine. "Let's see if we can figure out this little mystery."

But Plesur already had a plan. "We'll find out what they're doing up there," she promised. "And whoever they are, we'll make them pay."

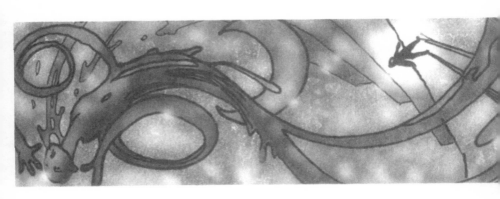

#

Chill winds blew across the grounds of the Kingston Police Academy. Rook stood in the courtyard with his graduating class, young, ready to change the world.

All his old friends were here. God, he hadn't seen them in years. His eyes followed the line of young officers. Berman and Franklin, always competing to be head of the class, real hotshots until they died in a botched drug bust. The top dogs of the academy mowed down on their first big case. Rook's heart was pounding in his chest. What the hell was going on here? He couldn't really be in Kingston, hair ruffling in the breeze, hearing

the applause of friends and family as each cadet marched to the stage.

"Rook?" a familiar voice called out.

Rook ran past the row of cadets, each staring off into space. Something was not right about them. Rook looked closer. Their skin had a strange glow, and behind each of their ears, small earbacks glistened like diamonds.

"Rook? That you, honey?"

He turned and entered his kitchen. The spicy smell of meat sauce filled his senses. He hadn't been in here in what, seven years? He reveled in the feel of his old apartment, the one he shared with—Rook dashed into the living room, half out of breath. "Marcie?"

"Of course, who were you expecting?"

"How can you be here?" This had to be a dream. But she looked so real. Her honey hair, lustrous and shining, just as he remembered it, the sweet smell of her skin, her deep green eyes . . .

"Life is hell, Rook."

His college sweetheart couldn't be standing in front of him. She had run off with an Internet-ad salesman to California, complaining that marriage to a cop was like sitting on a time bomb.

It felt as if ghostly fingers were flipping through his memories, pulling them out one by one and holding them up to the light like grainy strips of century-old film.

In the muted half-light, machinery winked and hummed on the cold tile floor. The steady beep of a cardiograph sent shivers up his spine. There in the hospital bed lay his father, dying.

Rook had been nine. He still remembered those Saturday afternoons, watching the Yankees, making mock bets. They spent a lot of time together, right until the end.

Yet here he was, cheeks hollowed and gaunt, body ravaged by the disease that ate him from the inside out. Rook moved closer. "Dad."

"There is much sorrow in the world, Son," his father said.

Tears were in Rook's eyes now. So much sorrow. It was hard to hold it all in his mind. A world filled with madness, cruelty, killing, and sometimes it seemed even the police were part of the horror.

Rook swung away, sickened at the sight.

"So, what we got?" Lindi MacEar leaned against his desk, sipping a steaming cup of coffee. He'd always thought that she was attractive, but you didn't say something like that to your partner.

"Crazy shit."

"Sangacha's case." Lindi was suddenly across the room,

fingers flying over the touch screen like buzzing bees. "Come on, boss, let's lay it out, go through the facts, just like you taught me."

Rook tried to hold his hand up, but his body was too heavy, he couldn't move. His thoughts spun for a moment, then seemed to gain traction. "Sangacha put a set of coordinates in Plesur's head."

"Why?"

"Something happened at that place. Something requiring national security to bury it. It's got to be connected to Taste Imperative. People get killed just for knowing those words."

"What do you think it could be?"

"Something from the old days of the Emergency. I found an ISS badge at Sangacha's apartment."

"What else does she know?" Lindi prompted.

"Names."

"Who?"

The office lights swirled, brightened into flares that seemed to shine directly into his brain.

"Lydia Trenchard and Dr. Ronald Clampen," he heard himself say.

"Trenchard and Clampen. That's interesting. Anything else?"

"No." Suddenly Rook didn't want to talk anymore.

"I hope she's okay, all alone, no one to protect her." Lindi's eyes were full of concern.

"Julia and David will take care of her."

"Who?"

Rook studied his partner. "MacEar, I already told you all this."

"So where did she go?"

"Don't know. We had planned to head north, check out those coordinates."

"I see." She fell silent and turned to regard the vast cloudscape and the endlessly setting sun behind them. "It's so beautiful, isn't it?"

Her face seemed to waver, hair flashing from brown to white, dark eyes melting into piercing blue.

He was standing on clouds. The sun was setting, permanently, and throwing flat beams, limning everything in gold. A choir was singing, somewhere close by, soft and low.

The golden light warmed the marble beneath his feet. Greek-style temples appeared, with a broad plaza below, connected by wide staircases. Then there were angels. Had to be. Ten feet tall, massive white wings, faces carved

in silver, with dark eyes that seemed to stare right through him. Those faces, he had seen them before. Faces of pleasure models.

For some reason Rook was walking up a set of stairs toward one of the temple-like structures. The sun played on the long line of white columns, sending shadows through the interior. A gentle breeze had sprung up, and the clouds began to move, flowing beneath and around the temples and the white marble surfaces.

"We all walk our own path to the gates of eternity."

"What are you doing to me?" Rook cried.

"I'm trying to help you," a chilly voice answered. "You want to do the right thing. That's why you joined the academy. You're smart, honest, made detective in record time. All to make sure the world is just."

"Right." Rook closed his eyes.

Suddenly she was there, standing at the top of the vast staircase. Radiant in a white gown, simply tied at the waist, with her hair pulled back partly from her face, Louisa

Marion was ageless, her eyes filled with the wisdom of time and the beauty of love.

She watched him as he approached and stood beside her. For a moment neither of them spoke, bathed in the glow of the distant sun.

"You've had to do questionable things. But you do not hate or act out of spite or fear." She reached out and took his hand in hers. "We live in a world of confusion and chaos. Wrong is right. Truth is fiction. Truth is lies. Sometimes we cannot see the light at the end of the tunnel."

His chest ached as he saw Plesur through the rain-streaked windows, running away because he had asked her to. Her blond hair a flash in the darkness.

"We must be guided by a higher purpose, working for a goal that is worth all we sacrifice. Do you have a goal, Detective?"

"I just want to do my job."

"You can save your country." She was so beautiful, so regal and calm, yet he sensed the sadness that beset her.

"Manuel understood that, once. He did what I asked because he knew it was necessary."

"And you murdered him," Rook said.

"No. We did not kill the general." She saw his stunned expression. "You have worked hard on this case, Detective." Her other hand came up to stroke his cheek. "But still you are unfulfilled, without purpose."

In the dark recess of his heart, he knew that to be true.

"This country needs someone to protect it, to guide it into the future," she told him. "I have done so, it is what I

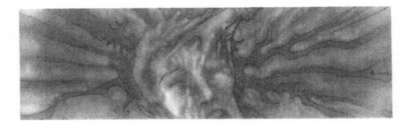

have lived for. And now people are trying to tear down all that I have accomplished. Do you know what that feels like, Detective? Watching as your life's work is destroyed?"

Rook listened, feeling as if he were being swept up in a great tide, something much larger than himself. She was a lighthouse, a beacon, standing alone against vast waves of malignant darkness. Something clicked into place, as if a piece of himself he'd forgotten had suddenly been restored. He wanted to help her.

"From here, you shall be reborn. An avenging angel to strike down all who oppose me." She touched his forehead in a blaze of baptismal fire, and Rook knew what he had to do. "We will make everything as it should be, as it is meant to be."

The clouds vanished, the marble disappeared. A metallic taste was in his mouth, then he felt consciousness slip away.

CHAPTER 19

"I'm sorry for your loss," Lydia Trenchard spoke from the video screen. "I wish there was something I could do."

The next morning, they were sitting with Rory in the center of the Calann clan's war room, a concrete bunker buried under a giant boulder just south of the house.

A half dozen big screens filled one end of the space, and four young Calanns worked at a pair of desks piled high with equipment, keeping close tabs on everything happening within miles of the fortress.

One screen was filled with different views down the highways that ran into the former proscribed zone. Rory had explained the clan had positioned upwards of two thousand Minicams in and around their territory.

Ingrid had expressed admiration for the quality of the secure line that Rory's phone geek had pulled up to call Lydia Trenchard.

"I've run the coordinates through several databases," Trenchard continued. "The facility was part of the aqueduct system that brought water down to New York City from the Catskills. But it's been closed for over thirty years."

"Then it became a proscribed zone," Jim informed her.

"Yes."

"But they stopped trying to enforce that," Jim added.

Lydia surveyed the group. "Ten years ago, the governor of New York confronted Marion about it. Actually threatened Sable Ranch to get the zone shut down."

"What happened?" Julia asked.

"He died."

"Convenient, like," said Jim with a mordant chuckle.

"So it's government property," Julia said. "What's the official explanation for what they're doing there?"

"All files have been removed or deleted," Lydia said.

"How can they do that?" asked David.

"Very easily," answered Jim, who handed a little data-stick to one of the men working at the main board. "Put this up on the screen, would you?"

"The fact the files have been removed doesn't necessarily mean there's something to hide," Lydia cautioned.

"Well, I'll 'ave to disagree on that one." Jim deftly tapped a remote keypad, displaying images across the screen. One by one, he enlarged them. "These are shots of the area six months ago. The fence was rusting out, holes the size of raccoons; signs all shot up."

The photos showed a concrete compound surrounded by sagging razor wire nestled under massive aqueduct pipes. Dense forest surrounded the windowless fortress, suggesting whoever built it had wanted to keep it hidden deep in the woods, away from prying eyes.

"Impressive surveillance." Lydia eyed Jim. "What did you say your line of business is?"

"Just a concerned citizen, ma'am." Jim smiled innocently.

"Very concerned."

"Now these shots were taken a few weeks ago," Jim continued, eyes gleaming. "New fence, new signs."

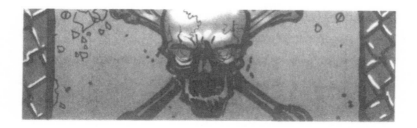

Shining coils of razor wire and fresh skull-and-crossbones signs warned potential intruders, and the road leading to the facility had been cleared of overgrown branches.

Lydia studied the images. "Open for business."

"In case you're still having doubts, meet this bloke, a brand-new guest to the area." Jim switched to a video image. For a few seconds there was just vegetation and small trees. Then they parted and a tall, bipedal machine emerged, loping across the field of view. The thing looked like an insect, seven feet tall.

Plesur had gone silent.

"Thunderclaw, Mark 3, I believe," said Jim.

"I'd say you're right about that," agreed Rory.

"I've seen that," said Plesur.

The giant robot moved purposefully around the perimeter, scanning the grounds for intruders.

"When Rook's house blew up, one of those things chased us." Plesur studied the screen. "I didn't have the upgrade then. But I remember that robot."

"Hard to forget," Julia muttered.

"It's waiting for me," said Plesur.

"Plesur, I know you want to find out what's going on, what Taste Imperative is," Lydia said. "But even with your earback, you can't get inside this place by yourself."

"She's right," Jim agreed. "Thunderclaw ain't there to meet and greet, darlin', it'd kill you as soon as it laid eyes on you."

"Then I can't be seen," Plesur reasoned. She pinned Jim with her determined blue gaze.

David put his hand on Plesur's shoulder. "You know what happened with that last robot. We have to think this through, come up with the best strategy."

"Eve gave me the paper you found at Sangacha's. Can't find anything on Taste Imperative and the names come up deceased, but I'll do everything I can," Lydia promised. "General Sangacha must have had good reason to give those coordinates to Plesur." Lydia looked over her shoulder as a knock sounded on her door. "I'm leaving for California to meet Paula Perez. I'll brief her on this latest development." Her connection winked out, leaving the room in silence.

"I ain't no rocket scientist," Jim whispered conspiratorially, "but I'll tell you this. Whatever it is they did in there, they're doin' it again."

Suddenly Plesur got up. "We have to find out."

"How can we do that?" Julia asked. "We can't get near the facility without alerting that monster."

"I don't know." Plesur didn't have that kind of information.

But Jim did. "Well, the doctor's been thinkin'. See, I know of another way into that place."

He switched to a satellite image of the area, zooming in to a crevice on the mountainside.

"We found this opening a while back, it's on one of the main fault lines through the mountain, and if you're thin

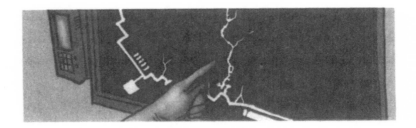

enough, you can wriggle in there. It's a maze inside, three-dimensional-like. There's ice caves, with ice that doesn't melt in the summer. We found that one of the side passages connects to this ventilation shaft. Very narrow approach, and the shaft goes down at a steep angle, but there are climbing pins set in the concrete, so they could send guys up to check it out, maybe clean it."

"How did they miss that?" Julia asked.

"Oh, they didn't. It was covered over with cement, but there was water running down the shaft, see, froze in the winter, thawed in the summer. Terrible for concrete, big chunk broke off."

"The robot won't see us go in the ventilation shaft," Plesur said.

"'Ang on," Jim said. "My two boys who went exploring, they never came back. Vanished. We went back every day for two weeks, found neither 'air nor hide of 'em. Completely vanished."

For a moment they were silent, thinking of two boys lost forever in the dark places underground.

Julia, Plesur, and David looked at one another.

"This is big, maybe too big for us," Julia said. "We don't have the artillery to bust into a top-security secret government compound. Plesur, maybe you did everything you were supposed to do. You had Lydia's name, now she knows everything. I don't know what else we can do."

"What if we're the only ones who can stop it?" asked David.

Julia glared at him. "You suddenly get a death wish?"

David shook his head. "Now that we know there's a back door, we could at least scout it out, see what's there."

"So," said Julia after a little while, "what you're suggesting is we sneak in underground?"

"Yeah. We have some equipment that'll help, too." Jim started to pace the room. "Climbing stuff, mostly. And some weapons. Actually, a lot of weapons."

"And when we get to this air shaft, then what?" Julia demanded.

"We send someone down to the bottom."

"See what's there," Plesur finished.

Julia met David's gaze. She recalled the TYGO, racing after them across the uninsured world. They'd been lucky to get away. Were they really ready to face something like that again?

"Best shot is a small group," said David.

Suddenly, Julia felt ashamed that she was more interested in running away. These two pleasure models, with barely a few years of existence between them, were ready to risk their lives for natural-born humans.

Julia sighed. "Let's go take a look."

The tiny radio box that Jim wore clipped to his shirt pocket spoke up.

"We got a 203. Found this guy walking on the road completely dazed."

"Where is he?" Jim spoke into the voice box.

"Out by the county road. Next to Fox Lake. Had a bit of a rough night by the look of him. Says he's a cop, Venner. Told me he's looking for a p-mod called Plesur."

"Rook?" Plesur went pale.

"What?" Julia blurted. "That's impossible."

Jim grinned at the trio. "Looks like your detective didn't want to miss the party."

"Rook alive?" The shock had driven Plesur back to monosyllables.

"But we saw ..." Julia realized they hadn't seen any-thing. They'd gone down the stairs, running for their lives, leaving Rook alone to face that thing.

"Where is Rook?" Plesur was on her feet, trembling.

"They're bringing him in," Jim said.

"But how did he get here?" asked David.

"I knew it. He didn't die!" Plesur tore open the door and ran outside.

CHAPTER 20

Riding in on the back of the ATV, Rook felt a kind of seamless joy. He'd made it. He'd been through hell and he was back. His face was still covered in scabs, his wounds were still deep and aching, but he was alive. He put a hand down and felt the reassuring weight of the sidearm.

The sun felt good on his skin, the air was sweet.

He couldn't quite remember where he'd been, or how he'd got here, but he knew that it didn't matter.

"It is a beautiful day," he murmured to himself.

The girl driving the ATV had dark hair in braids and wore a camo outfit. She had an assault rifle holstered on the front of the wagon, which she drove with the confidence of someone who'd grown up at the wheel.

The ATV swung down a narrow track. Branches whipped across their path and he had to duck, but then they emerged into a clearing with a farmhouse. Rows of crops grew off to one side, just beyond the porch. He didn't know where they were, but it seemed orderly and that pleased him.

And there was Plesur, running toward him, calling his name.

He got down. A wave of joy rose through him. Amid

golden beams of sunlight, a choir was singing, and a quiet voice said, "Do what you have to do."

Something was nagging at him, something about Plesur that he couldn't quite remember. But those thoughts were dark and annoying and Rook blotted them out of his mind.

And here was Plesur, coming right up to him, golden hair streaming behind her, tears of joy brimming in her bright blue eyes.

"Rook," said Plesur as she reached for him. "You're alive."
"Still kicking."

It was the most natural thing in the world. He raised the gun and pulled the trigger. Plesur fell backward in a spray of blood. He felt the warm droplets land on his arms, his face. Seeing the beautiful pleasure model lying on the ground, face stunned, eyes growing dark with pain, Rook felt a wave of satisfaction wash over him. It was good to have a purpose.

There was a scream, a shout, then something slammed into him and he was down on the ground. Someone was punching him, over and over, then the lights went out and

with them went the choir and the quiet voice and everything else.

CPSIA information can be obtained at www.ICGtesting.com
Printed in the USA
LVOW07s1940201014

409632LV00001B/30/P